Prologue: Wish Fulfillment

'*Eaargh!*', the demon screamed as the knight pierced through its body with his blade.

'*Good work, now all we need to do is complete the puzzle and split the loot.*', the ranger said, picking the locked door behind the demon's corpse.

"*Don't worry about the puzzle, I have a familiar that can solve the puzzle.*", the mage answered.

'*Man, if only someone like that existed in real life that had the solution to every problem I had. It'd make everything so much easier…*', the knight said.

'*Like some kind of guide?*', the mage asked. '*If something like that existed, I wouldn't work another day in my life hahaha!*"

'*I wouldn't want something that, telling me what to do, that'd be so annoying, like being a kid. What I'd want is a billion dollars, that way I could relax and play games all day hahaha.*', the ranger joked.

'Yeah, you'd look like a loser if you had someone standing behind you all day telling you everything to do.', added the mage.

'I dunno man, I'd rather just turn my brain off and let someone else take the wheel for a change.', the knight said.

'I feel you man, used to think the same thing but then life comes at you fast. Don't got time to think about any of that any more with all the work I have to do. Anyway I'm going to log off for now, have a meeting tomorrow.', the mage said before leaving.

'I think I'll go too. It's pretty late where I am and I have finals in a few weeks; I shouldn't be playing right now anyway.', the ranger replied before leaving as well.

The knight now alone also decided to log off as well. In reality, the knight was just a teenaged boy. The boy yawned before looking at the time. Half past midnight.

'If only something like that did exist.', he thought as he turned off his computer. His entire body ached as he got up from his chair and the dark circles under his eyes were visible even outside of the glow of moonlight shining through the window onto the floor of his room. He laid on his bed with his eyes closed, still awake. He was in another world in his mind, daydreaming about how much easier his life would be if a guide for life really did exist.

Despite having what one would consider a good dream, tears were forming in the corners of his eyes. Every night was the same. The boy would never admit it to anyone, but he knew how pathetic what he was doing truly was.

The boy knew what needed to be done, but he was too afraid to change. If only, he wished, someone would come save him from himself.

Chapter 1: The Bottom

The students were restless; They knew class was over soon and they would finally be able to go about their day. Nothing could contain their excitement; they were all discussing their plans after class with their friends. Everyone except an unkempt boy sitting silently in the middle of the classroom.

"Hey Mr. Anderson! You should dismiss us early since you're such a nice person!" one of the boys shouted from across the classroom. The teacher chuckled and replied, "You know they'll keep you inside until the bell rings anyway, do you want to stare at the doors that badly?", to which the students giggled gleefully.

"Oh well, you guys can go. By the time you get downstairs the bell will ring anyway. Except for you John, you have some work to do.", said the teacher, looking directly at the silent boy sitting in the middle of the classroom. John said nothing and laid his head on his desk.

"Is something the matter John?"

"He's always like that. A loser and an idiot, not to mention a dweeb. I don't think he even knows how to talk!", said the same boy from earlier. The others surrounding him erupted into laughter.

"Dylan!", Mr. Anderson said sternly to which the boy responded, "What? If it bothered him maybe he should tell me to stop!" John was still laying down on his desk, his eyes burning fierce with malice, but he didn't say a word. As the students began leaving the classroom, so too did John. "Hey, John! Did I not ask you to stay after class?" Mr. Anderson said. John turned around and sat back in his desk, not before mumbling a few curses under his breath.

"What do you want?"

"That's not how you talk to people John."

"I couldn't care less about 'how I talk to people' and I couldn't care less if you're going to berate me over it."

John began getting up from his seat until Mr. Anderson stopped him. "John, that's not what I was going to ask you. Your test grades are great, but you fail to hand in any assignments. Why?". John didn't bother to answer the question or even look in Mr. Anderson's general direction. Instead, he began picking under his fingernails.

Mr. Anderson let out a sigh, "Does it have anything to do with what just happened? Do you want to talk about it?". Suddenly John started smiling smugly, "I don't want to talk about it, bye." and ran out the door. "John, wait! You still have to..." the teacher tried to say, but it was too late. He was already out of earshot.

John was pleased by the small 'victory' he had over his annoying teacher and began jogging home. Mr. Anderson obviously didn't care; he was just asking because it was his job. Unfortunately, his little happiness wouldn't last so long. He didn't make it a block before someone grabbed the hood of his sweater.

"Where the heck do you think you're going, punk?". John turned around quick enough to move his head slightly before his face was greeted by Dylan's fist.

"How can I practice if I don't have my punching bag?", said Dylan, punching John in the gut.

"By the way John, what's with the holdup? Teach made you stay 'cause you're dumb as a rock?". As Dylan struck John across the face his underlings roared with laughter. The pain they inflicted upon John was just another way for them to entertain themselves. They were the popular ones, the strong ones. They saw everyone below them as their playthings.

The very thought of that made John furious, but he didn't have the strength nor the courage to stand up for himself. As far as he knew, the only option he had was to stand there and let Dylan pummel him like a punching bag until they were bored or distracted by something else. Coincidentally, a moment later one of Dylan's followers spoke up, "Oh crap, we only have twenty minutes to get to the concert!". Dylan immediately stopped beating John and threw him against the pavement, "Dang it I wasted too much time on this idiot, let's bounce!".

The bullies had gone, and with them so too was the small happiness John had. It wasn't the first time this had happened, nor would it be the last. John began dusting himself off and walked home. As he took off his sweater, he noticed the hood was slightly torn. *"Probably when he grabbed me, sadistic prick..."* he thought to himself. His entire body boiled with rage, why should he have to suffer? Why doesn't anyone want to help him? On his way home he was too angry to feel the pain from his bruises, too angry to think about anything but revenge. Nobody was home yet, which was normal for John. His parents were too busy with work and once they did arrive, they'd be too tired to do anything.

Once John flopped himself onto his bed not even bothering to change his clothes. Now that his anger was dissipating, he was too exhausted to do much of anything. After what had happened today, all he wanted was to go to sleep and forget everything. As the hours went by John was finally able to go to sleep, but he would never forget what happened today.

It was yet another day of school. *"Another meaningless day"* John thought to himself. Unlike his peers who were passing time with what he considered "mindless chattering", John had nothing to do while the class waited for their teacher to arrive. Normally John lays his head against his desk, but today he chose to observe the other students around him. The two in front of him were talking about some late-night cartoon. The guy to his left was panicking and trying to complete an assignment that was due today. The girl beside him was shuffling a deck of playing cards. Unfortunately for John, she saw him staring at her. Embarrassed, John looked away. He didn't want to look like a weirdo.

"Want to play a game, John?" the girl said cheerfully, placing cards on John's desk. He returned the cards, mumbling under his breath, "'m too busy, childish games, don't want to play". Despite what he said, John was very much interested in playing. In fact he was interested in everyone around him. He wanted to talk with the two kids in front of him about that cartoon, complete the assignment he also didn't complete with the guy right next to him, talk about a video game he played with anyone in the class. Instead, he chose to lay on his desk doing absolutely nothing. It wasn't what John wanted, but he spent so much time pushing everyone else away that it would have felt awkward for him to suddenly want to interact with others.

The entire day seemed to blur together for John. Doing nothing of value, paying little to no attention, spending most of his free time loitering in the stairwells and corridors alone. Had it not been for

Dylan's friends and their constant harassment, it would be difficult to tell if he was there or not. John hadn't realized it yet, but his life had become a routine. He spent his entire day spacing out in class, surviving the pain inflicted by Dylan and his lackeys, playing games, and sleeping in an attempt to forget everything that happened that day. The only thing that made John feel alive was his anger. There was some truth to John's thoughts. Every day was indeed meaningless, so long as he never tried to do anything to change it.

"So is that it? You're just going to let them bully you?", an unknown voice asked.

John didn't bother answering nor did he wonder who asked it. Surely, he thought, nobody was asking the bruised, unkempt, and friendless loser that was limping home.

"Wrong, I AM asking the bruised, unkempt, and friendless loser that's limping home", the voice said again.

Puzzled, he turned around to find whoever the voice belonged to. The man the voice belonged to was the most bizarre sight John had ever seen. A strange white robe tied around his waist covering a sickening shade of blueish-green clothing and if the clothes weren't strange enough, the man's skin was deathly pale with hair so black it seemed to absorb the light around it.

"So, do you enjoy living like beneath everyone?", the man asked again. John stared at the man, dumbfounded. Once he finally collected his thoughts he finally answered.

"Pfft-HAHAHAHAHAHA! Who the heck goes around looking like that!? Asking me questions when you should be asking questions about your sanity, you freak! Do you work at a circus or something?"

John had laughed so much that he couldn't breathe. Who the heck did this guy think he was, coming out of nowhere asking strange questions? Maybe there was a circus in town, but John wouldn't know or care. Laughing at that lunatic was enough to pick up his mood and forget the abuse he suffered today, so for the first time John decided to do his homework. Today was one of the few days when John didn't come home seething with rage, so why not make the best of it? For once in a very long time, John managed to go to sleep peacefully.

The next morning came soon enough. The cold from the wind seemed to rip through the student's coats, but it wasn't the cold that was making them shiver. All the students were thinking the same thought. Winter break is finally here! Whether it be discussing their plans with their friends or just daydreaming about them, every student was too distracted to focus on classwork. Or they were, until Mr. Anderson gave them each a folder filled with assignments.

"Those assignments are due the week you guys return from winter recess. Try not to lose them, it was not fun printing that many copies.", Mr. Anderson said, to which nearly every student groaned in unison. John, however, couldn't care less about the assignments. He knew Dylan and company were going to jump him after class and were guaranteed to take it. As the class was getting ready to leave, Mr. Anderson beckoned to John. John also knew that was also going to happen, so he pretended not to see it and left.

John barely made it to the end of the block before getting tackled by one of Dylan's lackeys. "Aww, what's the rush? You didn't even say 'bye'!"

The others took his bag and emptied it onto the pavement. Once they found the folder of assignments, they took it and destroyed it to the best of their ability while Dylan pummeled John into the pavement. Once they were finally satisfied, they gave John a few more kicks and left him on the ground with his belongings scattered about. John got up, his anger building with every notebook he picked up. More blood rushed to his head with every sheet of paper he put back into his bag. He was so angry that he couldn't even hear the footsteps approaching him.

"Are you okay John? Mr. Anderson asked me to give you an extra.", a boy handed John an extra folder. He would have recognized the boy as the one who sat beside him in class, but in his anger, John immediately snapped, "Piss off you idiot! I don't need your god damn help!", snatching the folder and pushing the boy away. They're all worthless scum. The ones who bullied him, the ones who stood by and did nothing. Every single one. One day they will get their comeuppance, and when they do, he would do the same they did to him.

But then… something crept into John's mind. A thought so terrible that it would make anyone despair. As his despair grew, the thought began echoing louder and louder, until he could no longer pretend it wasn't there.

'What if things never change? What if I never get my revenge? Will I always be their punching bag?'

John couldn't take it any longer. He ran up the stairs, opened a drawer in his desk, and pulled out a large knife. Death was a preferable alternative to being their victim forever. Thoughts began flooding his head. What about his parents, what would they think? Wouldn't stabbing himself be painful? But then, one single thought shone like a giant flaming beacon in the middle of his thoughts and with it, his anger ripped through his despair. The very thought of his bullies joking about his death made his blood boil and body shake with so much rage that he didn't even notice the pain in his hand from clenching the knife so hard. Eventually, John slammed the knife into the desk.

"Good choice.", said a voice behind him.

John stopped and immediately turned around. The only person who should be home right now is him, who could possibly have spoken? Standing behind him was the same bizarre man from the other day.

"Who the heck are you!? How did you get in here!? What do you want!?", John immediately yelled, jumping towards the door.

"Whoa! So many questions at once! Fine, I'll answer them. My name isn't important. How did I get in here? Easy, I snuck in.", the man began to smile.

"As for what I want… the same thing I asked you the other day. Do you enjoy living the way you are right now? Do you like being beneath everyone and tormented because of it?"

John was surprised. Who the heck was this guy? What kind of person breaks into someone's house just to ask them a question?

"You've seen those jerks beating me down. Who would enjoy being someone's punching bag?"

The man raised one of his eyebrows, as if he were surprised by the answer, "Oh? If you don't like being his 'punching bag', then why don't you ever do anything about it?"

"I would if I could. He has his friends with him. What can I do about six different people trying to rip me apart?"

"Without his friends he's still stronger than you, and even if that wasn't the case, just ask for help. Oh wait, you don't have any friends, and snap at anyone that shows you any kindness."

Who did this crazy guy think he was? What did he know about John's plight? Nobody was willing to help him, they're all just acting like they do. They're all worthless fakes. The man began frowning.

"Surely you aren't thinking something stupid like 'nobody actually wants to help me, they're all phonies.'"

"How did you know that!?", John said, dumbfounded. "Hahaha! Kids like you are idiots! You know people who want to help you, you're just too afraid to ask for it!", the man laughed.

"The only way you could help me is if you killed Dylan and his friends. Nobody's willing to do that, so nobody really wants to help!", John yelled at the man.

Then man stopped laughing and stared at John. "If they died, how would that change anything? Would their deaths allow you to be able to make friends? Would their deaths make you stop being a depressed antisocial loser?"

"Then what am I supposed to do? Ask a teacher to scold him for a few minutes so he can come beat me up even worse? That jerk's lucky he was born stronger than me. If it were the other way around, I'd tear him apart!"

"No! Stand up for yourself!", the man snapped at John. His anger with John's answers was clear on his face. "While you're sitting down here despairing or playing video games, he's studying to maintain his grades. While you're sitting alone thinking about revenge and spilling his blood, he's training for the football team! He wasn't "born stronger" than you. He puts more time into self-improvement than you've ever thought about it!"

"So!? Just because he 'puts in effort' means he's allowed to be a jerk!?", John responded, tears welling up in his eyes.

"No, it doesn't. What allows him to rip you apart day after day is you! You've done nothing to stop him! You don't even try! Why do you keep making excuses? what are you afraid of!? What could he possibly do to you that he already hasn't that prevents you from doing anything? Nothing!"

"So what am I supposed to do!?", John yelled back at the man, tears streaming down his face.

"You don't know what to do!?", the man suddenly grabbed John's shoulders and stared deep into his eyes, "If you don't know what to do, I'll tell you what to do! I'm not going to force you to do anything you hear me? Do you want to stop the bullying? Do you want to stand up for yourself? Do you want to change!?"

It felt as if the words were caught in John's throat. He wanted to say yes, but it was as if his entire body wanted to prevent him from doing so. "What's your answer!?", the man yelled at him.

"Y-yes…", John quietly mumbled.

"I can't hear you! Say it clearly!"

"Yes! Why would I not want to!?"

"Good, I'll see you tomorrow morning, complete your homework in the meantime.", the man said, leaving the room immediately after the last word left his mouth.

John stood there for what felt like an eternity. The man may have not thrown a single punch at him, but his words packed more power than any of John's bullies could ever have. Finally free from his daze, John ran out of his room to search for the man, but he had already disappeared as if he were never there in the first place.

"Where'd he go? Am I going crazy?", John thought aloud. Regardless of whether or not he was hallucinating, the words the man had said stuck onto John like splinters and they would make sure he would never forget his words for a very long time.

Chapter 2: The Beginning

"Up and at em, kid!", a voice yelled directly at John's ears. John barely had time to register what was happening before he rolled off his bed.

"Ow! What the- who's there? What's happening?", John yelped, wincing in pain from falling off the bed. As John rubbed his eyes, the figure in front of him became much clearer. It was the man from the other day. "Wh-what are you doing in here!?", John screamed, scrambling to get up and cover himself.

"I did tell you that I was going to come back in the morning, didn't I? It seems I've arrived at the right time. Now get ready, you have some work to do."

"Work? What are you talking about?"

The man snorted, "Don't tell me you've forgotten already! It was yesterday after all."

As John tried to remember what had happened the other day, he immediately covered his face with his hands. 'Oh my God, did I actually say all of that yesterday?', John thought to himself, mortified.

"Instead of dying from embarrassment, go wash your face, wake yourself up.", the man said. John reluctantly followed the man's orders and tidied himself up. Once he returned to his room, he immediately sat down on his chair and turned on his computer.

"What do you think you're doing?", the man said.

"What does it look like? There's nothing to do so I'm going to play a game."

"Weren't you going to improve yourself? Isn't that why I'm here?"

"Yeah, yeah. How about another day?", John said dismissively.

"Another day, and when that day comes, postpone it until another day. And then your break will end, and then you'll be at the mercy of Dylan and company once again. And then you'll complain that nobody wants to help you, and then you'll go back to- "

"Shut up!", John turned around to face the man who was smiling. "Tch, fine. I'll 'improve myself'.", he said sarcastically. John began stretching, and the man did nothing but watch. Once he finished stretching, he began to sit down.

"Wait, that's it? What happened to 'improving yourself'?"

"What? I did some stretches, that's good enough."

"That's nowhere near enough effort! You think stretching a bit is going to change anything? Drop down and give me twenty right- in fact, do as many pushups as you possibly can", the man said sternly.

"Twenty pushups this early in the morning!? Are you insane?", John exclaimed. He didn't want to exert himself so early in the morning. It's the first day of the break anyway, he wanted to relax and play some games.

"Do I look like I care? Start doing pushups until I tell you to stop, or I'll leave right now. Maybe I could tell Dylan all the juicy little secrets you told me. I bet they'll hurt more when he's pummeling you into the pavement with both his fists and your most embarrassing moments."

John's eyes went wide with fear, "You wouldn't dare!", but the man's eyes said everything. "A-alright I'll do the pushups, just don't say anything", John said weakly.

John's body wasn't accustomed to exercise. He had spent so long sitting behind a monitor that the only physical activity his body ever had to do was a bit of walking to and from school, carrying his bag, and maybe helping his parents when grocery shopping. Each pushup felt like a herculean task, his body screamed out in pain. After five pushups, John collapsed onto the floor, panting. But he could still feel the man's eyes, as if they were drilling a hole in his back.

"Did I tell you to stop? You barely managed to do five."

"I'm tired, I can't do any more pushups.", John gasped.

"'Oh please stop! I'm sooooo tired, won't you stop beating me? I'm a tired weakling that can only do five pushups before collapsing!', Is that what you're going to say to everyone that bullies? I don't know, it might work.", the man snickered.

The man seemed to know how to rile John up. Soon John's focus wasn't on the aching of his arms nor how many pushups he had done, but on his anger. "Keep going, you still have more pushups to do!", said the man, to which John complied. All he could think about was his hatred for Dylan, his contempt for his lackeys, and how his vengeance would be glorious. However, even his anger wasn't enough to keep him going. As soon as he ran out of steam, he collapsed yet again. This time however, John tried to keep going, but his arms had hit their limit. He couldn't even lift himself off the ground.

"Well you've managed to do a few pushups, barely.", the man said once he saw John was no longer able to do any more pushups. John barely managed to stand up before the man barked out his next order, "Fifty laps up and down the stairs, now!"

John's arms felt like lead. If his arms were to fall off at any moment, John wouldn't have been surprised. But John did as the man said. He ran up and down the stairs, over and over. The fatigue got to him, and he lost count. He forgot why he was running up and down the stairs. He forgot how tired his arms were. After fifteen or so laps, the man stopped him. He began saying something, but John was too tired to comprehend anything he was saying.

"Hey, get up! Don't lay down on the floor!", the man said loudly at John.

"Huh? Wha-? Oh uh, I need water.", John managed to say breathlessly. Now his legs were aching along with his arms, his mouth was parched, and his lungs felt like they were lit on fire. John lumbered towards the kitchen with the little energy he had to spare, and thirstily drank as much water as he possibly could. Afterwards he walked back to the living room and collapsed onto the couch.

"You're done already? That was only ten minutes!"

"Can't, too- too tired, can' barely feel myself!" John gasped. This was the first time he had ever exerted himself to such an extent. He was so tired he couldn't even speak coherently. "Jus'- jus' gimme a few minutes an' I'll be up". John glanced at the clock above him. As soon as he did, he groaned loudly. "Man, I promised my friends that I'd be online by ten for the event. Hey, uh- you never told me your name. You mind if I take a break for a couple of hours?"

The man chuckled before saying, "Remember what I said yesterday? I wasn't going to force you. Go ahead, play your games. Then you'll forget why you were exercising in the first place. And then the break will end, and then you'll go back to class, and then– "

"Okay, okay! I get it!", John said aloud before cursing the man in his thoughts. The man smiled to himself, as if he knew what John had just thought. But if he did, he didn't make any remarks about it.

"Now, let's see you run some more up and down the stairs, but carry those water bottles with you!", the man said, pointing at the pack of water bottles beside the kitchen door. John looked at the pack of bottles blankly. "Are you insane? How the heck am I going to carry that up and down the stairs?", he said angrily.

"How the heck will you ever stand up to anyone? How the heck will you ever change? When will you quit with these pathetic excuses? You won't change overnight, stop thinking you will". John began grumbling as he tried to lift the water bottles. He immediately regretted it. If his arms felt like they could have fallen off after the pushups, the water bottles felt like they could rip his arms off if he tried to carry them. John immediately dropped the bottles back down, it was painful enough to pick them up, but to carry them up and down the stairs? Impossible.

"Hey, did I tell you to put them down? You didn't even try!"

"I can't pick it up, they'll rip my arms off!"

The man shook his head, "You're right, you can't do anything. Maybe I should leave. I wonder if Dylan would appreciate knowing how much of a loser you are". John tried his best to restrain his anger, "Oh, you want to see me pick that up? Here, take a good look!", and he picked up the water bottles. The pain would have been too much to bear, but John wasn't focused on the pain. Grumbling incoherently, he climbed the stairs with the pack. *Damn him and his stupid water bottles and his stupid running. I have a billion other things I could do right now!*, John thought to himself.

It wasn't very long until John became far too tired to carry it up the stairs. He sat down at the base of the stairs, looking towards the man to see whether it was enough for him. The man wasn't even looking at him, he was laying down on the floor with his hands behind his head, as if he were resting. "You made me do all that, and you weren't even watching!?", John yelled at him.

"I made you do that? Ha! I told you that I wasn't going to force you to do anything. You did that all on your own!"

John could barely contain his anger at this point. "Fine. Then I'm going to eat something, I'm starving!" Despite saying that however, John looked towards the man yet again to see if he would say anything. But the man said nothing. He just laid on the floor with his eyes closed, smiling. "I'm going to go eat, you aren't going to say anything about that are you?", John asked the man. But the man stayed silent. "Hey, can you hear me? I said I'm going to eat; you aren't going to say anything about that?", yet the man stayed perfectly quiet. '*Whatever the heck that means*', John thought to himself, before heading towards the kitchen.

John rarely ate breakfast, and rarely would he ever finish his breakfast. Every day, his parents would cook breakfast for him, but he would never eat much and threw away most of it. Today however, he was famished beyond what he could ever imagine. He hungrily scarfed down every single scrap, but his hunger craved more. Only after devouring the lunch his parents had left for him did his hunger finally subside. John leaned against his chair, content.

"Wow, the way you inhaled all that made it look delicious!" John quickly turned around to see the man standing in the doorway. John quickly scrambled to his feet, wiping his face and putting his dishes in the sink, "Oh, uh you're still here? I'll get ready, just let me wash the dishes and stuff...". As John began to wash his dishes, the man sat in the seat John had just left.

"So, how do you feel now? Invigorated?"

"Invigo-wha? Also why are you asking?"

"You should already know. By the time you're done doing the dishes you should be ready to do some more exercise!", said the man, to which John groaned.

"Really? I've been working out for like an hour, that should be good enough for a day."

"Thirty-five minutes actually. You spent quite a bit of that time groaning and laying on the floor pretending to be tired, so you've only really been exercising for about twenty-five or so minutes."

"Alright, fine. Just give me a few minutes to r- ".

"Nope!", the man interrupted. "You're getting ten minutes to wash those dishes and you're going to be lifting that box up and down.", he said, pointing at a small, opened crate full of potatoes. Just looking at it made John's arms ache.

"What!? I thought you said you weren't going to make me to do anything!", John exclaimed.

"I said I wasn't going to force you, and I'm not. You can easily ignore what I'm saying and go play games, or go to sleep, or whatever else you want to do. I guess you didn't want to change after all, huh? Maybe Dylan will be much more inclined to listen to what I have to say!", the man said.

"How the heck is that not forcing me!? You're clearly using him to get me to work out!", John shouted.

"I have no idea what you're talking about!", the man said. "And even if I was, why are you saying that like what I'm doing is bad? So what if your body is aching a bit? Better that than rotting away behind your monitor all day."

"Oh man, here it goes. 'Video games are bad for your health! You need to eat your veggies and read books all day! You need to be a boring person that spends his time watching paint dry, entertainment is bad for you!'", John mocked.

"Hah! There's nothing wrong with entertaining yourself. What's wrong is complaining about others who don't. You think they're dullards who only lift heavy objects, but they also have hobbies. Hobbies they chose to spend less time on to improve themselves. They didn't reach that point overnight.", said the man.

John's head was beginning to hurt. *'How is that not contradicting what he had said earlier?'*, he thought to himself. The man immediately responded as if he could read his mind.

"You're probably thinking what I said was contradictory, but you're forgetting one thing. Those people have discipline, they know what restraint and moderation is. You don't. The second you get back to playing games is the second you forget why you were exercising in the first place".

"Well you don't have to be a preachy jerk about it", John muttered under his breath.

"Preachy?", the man remarked, surprising John who thought he couldn't hear him. "You're right, Maybe I am being overly preachy. And what of it? I'm still right. If not, prove me wrong right now… You see? You can't. Now if you're done complaining, finish washing your dishes and pick up that crate".

John was a little peeved by the man's response. He had absolutely nothing to say that could have refuted what the man just said. But he wasn't going to not listen just to spite the man. As John began lifting the box, the man started speaking.

"You spend so much time obsessing over Dylan. Do you think he does the same for you? You spend so much time pitying yourself. Why not find something better to spend that time on?" John tried to ignore him, but he kept asking questions.

"You're always trying to evade talking with other people, yet you're depressed about the fact that you are friendless. Why? Because of the "image" you've spent so long cultivating? Do you honestly think people care that much?"

John opened his mouth in an attempt to say something until he was cut off by the man. "I don't expect you to answer my questions. I want you to think about them. That's another problem of yours. Whenever someone tries to ask you something, you're so quick to dismiss it! Why? Some people want to help you, but you don't allow it. Not everyone is an evil backstabbing monster that wants to make you suffer."

"Okay, Mr. Self Help Book. I'll try to talk with others more and be a good person and blah blah blah and everything will turn out okay!"

"You see? You hide behind snarky cynicism whenever someone points out something you don't like or tries to help you. Why? What do you gain from doing that?", the man shook his head, "Absolutely nothing. You're too young to be that jaded. If you're so worried about how others perceive you, why don't start by working on that?"

"But I thought you said people don't care about my image? You're contradicting yourself again!", John blurted out. He saw an opportunity to prove the man wrong and immediately leapt at it. The man shook his head "They don't, at least not as much as you think they do, but you know who does? You. You're the one who's worried about how others see you, and if you see yourself as a friendless loser nobody wants to be around, you will treat yourself as such."

"Don't tell me you're still hung up from what I said earlier, are you?", the man said, silently laughing. Embarrassed, John remained quiet. He was too embarrassed to care about how much time had went by until the man finally told him to stop. Once he did, the fatigue seemed to flow into him like a dam exploding. He clung to the walls as his legs gave way, but his arms also felt like they've been lathed. The man looked up at the clock, smiling. "Wow, you've lasted longer than I thought! …". John was too exhausted to comprehend what the man was saying. He barely managed to drag himself to the couch before falling to sleep.

"…John… John!", a voice said, waking John from his slumber. As his eyes opened, he saw that it was his mother that had woke him up. "mmm? What time is it?", John yawned. He had been asleep for quite a while. "It's five minutes until six o'clock… what's that smell?", his mother said, "John, go to the bathroom right now and take a shower. You smell horrible!"

"Huh? I don't know what you're… oh", John said. He smelled himself and the stench hit him. His sweat had dried while he was asleep and laying in one place that entire time allowed the stench to build up. John began moving towards the bathroom, but he still felt exhausted from earlier despite resting. It took all the energy he had just to make it to the bathroom, and even more to undress, wash himself, change clothes, and destroy his dinner, but he did it anyway. Once John got to his room, he fell onto his bed and immediately fell asleep. For the first time since he could remember, John fell asleep soundly.

"Wow, that was the first time I've seen him eat like that. He must have been starving!", John's mother thought aloud.

"Strange, right? Plus he slept during the day. He hasn't done that since he was a child!", his father said, looking through the trash. "Look, he hasn't thrown out any of his breakfast or lunch either!"

"Something might be wrong, think we should ask him tomorrow?", his mother said, worried. His father felt the opposite, "If anything, something must have gone right. He finally managed to work up an appetite. Normally he eats like he hates eating, but today he ate as if it were his last meal!"

"Don't worry, he's probably just been working out. If something is wrong, we'll know.", his dad said.

The next day couldn't come soon enough. John's room was silent, except for the ticking of the clock on his dresser. *'Seven o'clock huh? Guess I slept a lot yesterday.'*, he thought to himself. This was the first time he had woken up so early, his parents were most likely leaving for work right now. Suddenly the door to his room opened, and his mother entered.

"Oh you're awake early. Are you okay? You looked very exhausted yesterday. Do you need anything? Water?", his mom asked.

"Uh, no. Why? Is something wrong? Did something happen?" John asked back, surprised by all the questions that were thrown at him.

"You see? There was nothing to worry about. The boy's doing fine. We don't need to bother him over every little thing.", his father said as he walked through the doorway.

"What's going on? Did something happen?"

"Oh nothing, your mother was worried that you may have been feeling under the weather. Speaking of weather, it's not very cold today, you could go hang out with your friends!", his father said, leaving the room.

"Have fun, John. If you stay home, remember to not open the door to any strangers or answer any phone calls from numbers you don't recognize!", his mother said, closing the door and running after his father.

"Why didn't you tell your parents that you don't have friends?", a voice said. John immediately sat upright. The man from the other day was there. "How the heck did you get behind the door!? Why are you there anyway?". John whispered to the man. "I snuck in behind your parents, and as for why I'm here? You already know that.", the man replied. He began stretching and beckoned towards John to get up.

"Come on, my body is still aching from yesterday. There's no way I'll be able to do anything today.", John said feebly. The man seemed not to care and began doing pushups. "So what are you going to do then? If your body's aching that badly surely you wouldn't be able to get up from bed, right?"

"Yes, I wouldn't be able to get up from bed, so could you leave me alone for today?", John said. If he could get the man to leave, maybe he could play some games today! The man immediately responded, "And if your body's aching to the point where you can't get up from bed, surely you wouldn't be able to play games right?"

"Oh come on! Give me a break, let me just play a little.", John pleaded.

"Very well, if you manage to push yourself like you did yesterday, then I'll stop pestering you for the rest of the day. Deal?", the man said.

John groaned loudly, "Fiiiine, I will. But you'll keep your word, right? You'll stop pestering me for the rest of the day?"

"That's up to how much effort you put in today."

"So it's a deal.", John began to smile. He was an expert at pretending to put in a lot of effort. It was how he managed to pass every P.E. classes with minimal effort. Luckily, he wasn't lying about his body aching, so it'll be even easier for him to fool the man into thinking he's giving his all. John got up and began stretching, contorting his face in anguish to show how much pain he was in. Once he finished his "stretches", he began his act. With every pushup he exaggerated the pain in his arms. With every sit-up his face showed all the pain he was suffering from. With every squat, he would stumble from "exhaustion" and grumble about how weak his legs felt from the other day. Once he finally completed his act, he laid on his bed complaining about how tired he was.

"Impressive. Very well done, John.", the man praised. 'Yes, he's buying it!' John thought to himself. Once the man was gone, John would be able to spend the day playing his games. *'Just a few more seconds and he'll be gone!'*, John thought to himself gleefully.

"You've put in effort alright. The effort you gave on that ten-minute act was indeed impressive. Effort that you could have easily given on actually exercising. Unfortunately for you, I'm not as easily tricked as your underpaid gym teacher.", the man continued. "But that wasn't the agreement. Looks like I'll get to annoy you some more today!"

"If I really was pretending, why didn't you say anything earlier?", John replied, still trying to feign exhaustion.

"You're not very good at acting. You also haven't said anything about eating breakfast, or washing your face, or any of the other excuses for that matter, not like they would have changed anything.", the man said, continuing his stretching and beckoning John to get up once more. "I already knew you were pretending, I just wanted to see how far you'd take your little charade."

John rose up once more from his bed, grumbling under his breath about how annoying the man was and how he needed to use the bathroom. Once John got back to the room, the man stood up. He didn't say a word, but John knew he wanted him to start exercising. As John started, the man began to speak.

"You said your body's aching, how about we talk about something to distract you from the pain?", the man said.

John, in the middle of a set of sit-ups, replied, "Talk about what? I know nothing about you, not even your name."

"Huh, I guess I haven't told you my name yet. It's Smith.", the man replied, but John's questions didn't stop there.

"So why are you doing all this? You just sneak into people's houses and pester them over strength training?", John asked.

"Any normal person would've asked that a long time ago. Some random guy snuck into your house and now you're questioning my motives?"

"Well, I didn't notice anything important missing, and you haven't killed me yet. So what do you gain from making me exercise?"

"Something like that. I'm a ghost that helps the downtrodden like you rise from the bottom."

"Cut the act, ghosts don't exist. Plus you said you snuck in, if you were a ghost couldn't you just go through walls?", John replied. "Besides, how is forcing someone to strain themselves 'helping' them in any way? Wouldn't it be easier to get rid of whatever, or whoever is causing their problems?"

Smith tilted his head slightly, as if he were deciding whether or not to respond to John. "Do you really want to know?", he finally responded.

"I make pathetic, worthless trash like you rip apart the excuses they use for not facing their problems. Strength training? Once you're done, you'll no longer be able to use your weakness as an excuse.", Smith finally said. "Huh?", John replied. He was stunned by that answer. His mind was trying to comprehend what Smith had just said, but Smith wasn't done talking.

"And it won't stop there. It won't stop until you no longer have any excuses to hide behind. If you choose to wallow in self-pity and despair after that, well I guess you want to stay a pathetic loser."

"Wh-What!? I… what!?", John was stunned by a mixture of surprise and anger. He wanted to strike the man with as much force as he could possibly muster, but he was too angry to move! No insult could compare to what Smith just said. He began to smirk, "Oh, are you angry? So what are you going to do about it?"

"Aww, is widdle baby going to throw a tantrum?", he taunted.

"I am NOT a pathetic loser! Raaaaaaaagh!", John yelled, before diving at Smith, only for phase right through him and crash directly into the wall. Smith began cackling loudly, "Aww, is widdle Johnny boy upset? Gonna cry?". John was trying to comprehend what just happened; did he really just go through Smith!? No, that's impossible. Ghosts don't exist, he probably just missed. John got up and began flailing his arms at Smith. "Aaargh!", he yelled, but his hands just went through Smith.

"What!? How!?"

"I told you, I'm a ghost. Are you done throwing your tantrum?"

"Why the heck should I listen to you then!? You can't do anything if you're a ghost!"

"That may be true", Smith replied, "But it's in YOUR best interest to listen. What do I possibly gain from making you exercise? Absolutely nothing". John glared at him menacingly, but he knew he was right. Regardless of whether or not Smith was a ghost, a person, or a hallucination, he would gain nothing from making John exercise. Begrudgingly, John decided to listen to Smith. This time however, neither of them exchanged words with each other. Smith sat calmly, watching John. John on the other hand was frustrated beyond belief. Every single one of his thoughts became unintelligible gibberish but shared one thing in common, hatred towards Smith.

John's rage wouldn't sustain him forever though. As the dam of his anger broke, the flood of exhaustion overwhelmed him. John could barely manage to move before Smith stood up. He stared at John, as if waiting for him to get up once more. John didn't get up, or rather, he couldn't get up. He laid on the cold floor, spent. "Is that good enough?", croaked John between gasps of breath.

"Well it seems you've managed to hold up your end of the deal, so I'll do the same.", Smith said, and disappeared. 'Thank God, he finally left…', John thought to himself. Maybe he could finally play some games… but then his stomach growled, he needed to eat! He carefully crawled down the stairs, limped across the living room, and hobbled into the kitchen. Once John devoured everything, he felt alive once more.

"Finally!", he yelled. Now it was his time! His parents weren't coming home any time soon, that dreaded Smith wasn't coming back any time soon, and he was no longer exhausted. He climbed the stairs, ran straight into his room, and immediately leapt into his chair. Today he could do what he wanted…

"…John…John are you okay?", a voice said. "Mmm? Wha- I fell asleep?" John said, surprised. The one who woke him up was his mother. 'Oh man did I really fall asleep again!?', he thought to himself.

"John… is everything okay?", his mother asked once more.

"Huh- oh yeah

, I'm fine. Just a little tired from working out.", John replied, yawning loudly. "You don't need to worry so much."

"If you say so… well don't push yourself too hard."

As she left the room, John started beating himself up mentally. 'Stupid, stupid, stupid! How the heck did I fall asleep!? Wasted an entire day dang it!', John thought to himself. A few moments later, his father walked in on him tugging at his hair. "Rough day?", John's father said as he sat on the corner of his bed silently with his hands clasped together.

"Not really.", John answered, assuming his father was waiting for his reply. "Just beating myself over the fact that I fell asleep."

"Why? Did something happen?", he replied with the slightest hint of concern in his voice.

"Ah, no, nothing happened. I fell asleep and felt like I wasted an entire day, that's it.", John replied hastily. John's father began to smile, "It's okay, you didn't waste the day. Don't push yourself too hard or your mother will start worrying."

'*What do you mean I didn't waste the day?*', John thought to himself. He didn't do anything today other than work out and sleep, how was that not a wasted day? He could have made a lot of progress in that new area that was recently added to the game he played. Before John could think about what his father meant, his popped into his room once more.

"Oh, you should probably shower before dinner.", his father said before leaving once more. '*Oh, that makes more sense.*'. John quickly washed himself and ate his dinner before finally falling asleep once more. His parents however, stayed up later once more to discuss what had just happened.

"You see? We didn't need to worry. He's just exercising a bit. Maybe he saw an image of a bodybuilder or something and wanted to look like that.", his father said happily.

"But what about his studies? If he spends so long asleep and working out, he won't have enough time for his homework.", his mother said.

"You give the boy way too little credit. I'm sure he knows to do his homework and such before exhausting himself like that. If it ever gets to the point where we need to help, we'll be there. But for now, let's give the boy a little privacy."

"I hope you're right…"

Chapter 3: Snow

"Up an at 'em, kid!", shouted Smith.

However, John was already up. Seven days had passed since he first saw Smith and, in that week, so has his routine. No longer did he wake up at noon just to pass time playing games until he was tired once more. Now he woke up at eight with his trusty "alarm clock" Smith to exercise a few hours before spending the rest of the day playing games. Ever since he begrudgingly accepted that Smith was indeed trying to help him, John suppressed his anger towards him. Having spent so long pushing his body to its limit was enough for him to forget about his vengeance on Dylan for the time being, even on the days he rested. John had already forgotten why he had started this journey in the first place.

"Come on! One more set, you did two more sets yesterday!", shouted Smith.

"I'm TRYING! Stop shouting at me!", John replied angrily through gritted teeth.

John had made considerable progress since he first started. Through his effort, John managed to build the stamina to exercise longer. Through Smith's scathing remarks, he managed to stoke his anger long enough to dull the pain. The struggling of the first few days were gone. The complaining of the first few days were also gone. What filled the void was the drive to become stronger.

"Okay, stop!", Smith shouted. John finally collapsed onto the floor, breathing heavily. "That's enough for now. I'll be back tomorrow.", Smith said before disappearing. John picked himself up from the ground, drenched in sweat. After taking a shower and replenishing his energy, he quickly raced back to his room to turn on his computer.

"Oh, the Knight is finally online!", the ranger said.

"Finally, let's get to the event area! I heard there's new weapons for mages. Would save a me a ton of time to get it now than pay someone for it.", the mage replied.

"Alright! Let's get going before my drop enhancer runs out!"

"Hey, Knight. You haven't said anything yet. You okay?", the ranger asked.

"I'm fine, just a bit tired. Gotta take it easy and all that you know?", John replied, but then the ranger asked again. *"You sure? You said that yesterday. Nothing wrong in real life?"*

"Who are you, my mom? I've just been working out recently to get into shape.", John answered. *"Ah, normal people things hahaha."*, the mage typed.

"Yeah yeah, let's just get on with the farming. I want to get that new lance, I heard it's really good!", John replied.

As John began hacking and slashing at fictional monsters with other players in the game, time flew by. What felt like an hour was actually three hours, but John didn't really care. He had completed all of his assignments for the break, he had exercised, he washed himself. He had done everything that's usually asked of him, so now was his time.

"By the way Knight, have you read this forum post? It's really funny.", the mage asked.

"No, why? What's it about?", John replied. *"It's just some posters screaming about the blizzard that's going to happen tomorrow. Hope they're ready to shovel a foot and a half of snow hahaha!"*, the mage answered.

As John started reading the posts on the forum, his heart immediately sank. The blizzard was going to hit his city… *'Dang it! Now my parent's will be home tomorrow…'*, he thought to himself.

"Pretty funny huh?", the mage asked. *"Yes, real funny. It'd be funnier if the storm weren't hitting my city directly."*

"Wait, the blizzard is going to hit your city? Hahaha that's hilarious! Good luck getting outside tomorrow hahaha!", the ranger replied.

"You should probably prepare so you're okay once you get snowed in hahaha.", said the mage.

John quickly logged off before realizing he had no way of actually preparing. At most he could tell his parents about the storm, but they would already know. Not a moment later, he heard his parents entering. As he rushed downstairs, he saw they were both covered with snow.

"Wha- did the blizzard start already?", John said, surprised.

"It's going to be snowing for quite some time. Hope it's only a foot. I really don't want to shovel three feet of snow just to pull out of the driveway…", his father said, shaking bits of snow off his coat. His mother had already rushed into the bathroom. "Brrr, it's freezing! You've been sitting alone in this cold?", his father said, shivering and turning on the heat.

"Well, I didn't feel so cold since I was exercising. Sorry.", John muttered, to which his father sighed, "You shouldn't apologize, John. If you didn't need it that's okay. You weren't wrong and it's not your fault."

The rest of the day carried on as usual. John ate his dinner and went back to his room. After a few stretches he laid on his bed and went to sleep. While he slept, the snow piled, and piled, and kept piling. It piled much higher than the twelve inches his father hoped for. Two feet of snow buried the sidewalks, buried his father's car, and covered the door.

The next day it wasn't Smith that woke John up, it was his father's anguish. John quickly tiptoed downstairs to see if anything was wrong. John saw his father attempting to open the front door just to get outside, but the weight of the snow pushing against the door was proving itself to be quite a formidable foe. Once he had finally managed to open the door, more he began cursing under his breath and began shoveling.

John began heading upstairs. He began to pull the covers over him until a small voice began whispering in his head. "Why don't you go help your dad?", the voice said. *'But it's freezing out there, and there's so much snow. I don't want to go…'*, he thought, pulling the covers over him. "But he's out there alone, shoveling all that snow. Don't you think your father wasn't also complaining about the cold?",

the voice responded. John reluctantly got up from his bed and changed
to clothes to withstand the freezing wind.

"Oh you're going to help your father? You didn't eat breakfast
yet!", his mother asked.

"It's okay, it'll taste much better after we're done.", John
replied, putting on his boots. As soon as he opened the front door, he
immediately regretted his decision. The freezing wind almost instantly
blasted his face with cold air and snow. The warmth and meal waiting
for him indoors was definitely much more inviting compared to
withstanding the harsh wind and wading through knee-deep snow, but
he had already made his choice and he wasn't going to change it so
soon.

"John is that really you? Are you sure you can handle
shoveling?", his father asked.

"Yes, I can handle it. Plus it'll be much faster if I help."

They began shoveling, and shoveling, and kept on shoveling.
And even more shoveling! When would the shoveling end!? At this
point, all the snow they removed had formed a giant mound. John and
his father wasn't ready to give up yet. With their combined effort they
had finally managed to clear enough snow to move easily. The mound

of snow created by all the snow they had shoveled resembled a miniature mountain.

"Thanks a lot, John. Really saved me a lot of time with your help.", his father said. Both of them were extremely exhausted from all the snow that they had just moved.

"You know, you're much stronger than you look. A few weeks ago, you would have never attempted to shovel snow like that!"

"You really think so?", John asked, blushing.

"Of course, you look much more confident. Well, when you're not blushing hahaha!"

"You didn't have to say the second part", John muttered, pulling his scarf up to cover his face.

"Tell you what, since you've helped me so much, do you want anything?"

"What?"

"Maybe some new clothes? A new game? Allowance?"

"Oh, uh I don't really know what I want", he answered. "I just came here to help a little, that's all."

John's father began laughing, "Really? You came out here just to help? Well, you can always change your mind!".

Once John returned home, the heat defrosted his face completely and brought feeling back to his frozen body. Unfortunately, the heat also made him realize how much his body ached from spending all that time in the cold shoveling snow. After scarfing down his breakfast to the best of his ability, John dragged himself up the stairs and immediately threw himself onto his bed. Laying down on the mattress was enough for his body to finally relax.

"So I guess it's a job well done huh?

John's body shot up the moment he heard that voice, only to fall back down and wince in pain. He turned his head slightly to the side to see Smith squatting and looking at him. At that moment he finally understood the voice from earlier.

"It was you!", he whispered angrily as to not alert his parents.

"Took you long enough to catch on. You think someone's thoughts just speak to them like that? You'd have to be crazy!", Smith cackled.

"So what? Do I need to do a billion and a half pushups to appease you, O mighty evil spirit?", John said sarcastically.

"No. I'm just here to laugh at you."

"Go away then! Let me rest you jerk!", said John as he tried to swipe at the man, only to strain himself further. Smith began laughing harder and disappeared as quickly as he arrived. '*Finally… peace and quiet…*', he thought to himself. The day carried on as usual, and as day became night, John finally retired to his room. The weather, however, doesn't sleep. As he slept, the blizzard made short work of all the effort he and his father had put into clearing it all out.

"… and shine, John!", his father said. John's eyes barely opened but he was awake.

"Mmm?", he said drowsily.

"Do you want to help me shovel snow again?", his father said, smiling. With all the additional snow to shovel, he had an excuse to spend some more time with his son. John on the other hand, was not happy at all.

"Ugh, didn't we do that yesterday?", he complained loudly.

"It snowed again last night. But it's fine right? We can just clear it again!", his father responded, this time with less enthusiasm. "I dunno… seems like a waste of time if it's going to snow again."

"All right…", his father replied. The disappointment in his voice was clear. John laid on his bed as his father left alone. Not a moment later after the door closed, Smith appeared with a wide smile on his face.

"Why didn't you help your father?"

"Why should I? The snow's just going to undo everything we would have done anyway, no point going…"

"So why did your dad go to clear it out if the snow is just going to undo everything he would have done?"

"How should I know? I'm too tired to think about that stuff, and today's a rest day…", John replied, turning over and pulling the covers over his head.

"You're just going to let your dad shovel all that snow?", Smith asked. John didn't budge.

"In the cold?". No response…

"For hours on end…". Still, no response…

"Alone…? Surely, a lonely person like you would understand, right?". John slowly poked his head out. "If I go, will you leave me the heck alone!?", he whispered through gritted teeth. Smith smiled, and left John alone. Cursing under his breath, John began preparing to help his father. After rushing downstairs he slowly opened the door, but that didn't stop the wind from blasting him with the freezing cold. It would have been enough to deter him from going outside but he had no choice. He had already promised Smith that he would help his father, so he braced himself.

"John, you came to help?". His father's face seemed to lighten up.

"I didn't say I wasn't.", he responded.

"Thanks John. I'd cry tears of joy if my tears wouldn't freeze onto my face", his father laughed. Energized from the thought of spending more time with his son, John's father began shoveling much harder. The snow that had piled up seemed to disappear in the blink of an eye with their combined effort. What felt like an eternity the day before seemed to pass in the blink of an eye today.

'Not as bad as I thought it would've been', John thought to himself. As the pair finally cleared out the last bit of snow, they began heading home. Despite being tired from clearing away so much snow, his father seemed very pleased.

"Thanks, John. You might not understand how happy you've made me, but I really am grateful for your help."

"Huh? You're freaking me out here dad…"

"Oh I am? Hahaha! Sorry about that. Now, did you think about what you wanted from yesterday?"

"Not really? It's just, I really don't know what I 'should' ask for."

"You don't need to put that much thought into it, just ask for what you want! Maybe a game, or a new whatever."

"I dunno, maybe some weights?"

"Well, that wasn't the answer I expected!", his father laughed. "We can go buy some together later."

The day went by as usual, but John's father was much more joyful than usual. John rarely spent time with his parents, but today was the first day he had actually lost track of time spending it with his family! Time that could have been well spent playing games! Strangely enough, he was fine with that.

John slept soundly that night. His father on the other hand, didn't. He was crying his eyes out in the living room. But they weren't tears caused by sorrow, they were tears of happiness! For many years, John's father was worried for his son. He was thirteen, yet he never mentioned any friends, never brought anyone home, rarely talked, barely ate, and always stayed confined to his room. But recently he had been changing. No longer did he look like a frail, fragile child that would break easily. No longer did he look like the husk of a person he used to. In the past few days alone he managed to interact with John for the longest period of time he has ever had since he was a child.

For the first time ever, John's father was proud of his son. Proud enough to believe his own words. Proud enough to finally be able to place his faith in his son.

Chapter 4: A Fresh Start

The entire room was deathly quiet, save for the ticking of a clock. John was wide awake but didn't move a single muscle. He could feel the end of the break approaching and it made him restless. Two and a half weeks, spending upwards of five hours spread throughout the day, he had spent pushing his body to the limit. The end result? Subtle musculature, an aching body, and slightly higher self-esteem. Not what he was expecting, but it's a start. But that wasn't what bothered him. He couldn't clearly remember why he started working out, something that had to do with the school. As he laid in his bed he kept thinking, but he couldn't remember what. Or maybe, he didn't want to remember it. Either way it was eating away at him and his sleep.

He laid there for what seemed like an eternity. He laid still as night turned to dawn and the first rays of sunlight began shining through his window. Like a boulder, he laid unmoving as his parents began moving about downstairs, preparing to leave for their jobs. Only when his alarm began ringing did he finally get up. John would have given up anything to just collapse back into his bed and go to sleep, but he knew that going to school would give him the answers he wanted.

John was almost entirely distracted on his way to school. What could possibly bother him to such an extent. Once he made it to the school, he still didn't feel like he knew what was going on. John was quite early for today, one of the first to arrive. The halls were empty save for the echoing of his footsteps. He sat in his seat and began tapping his shoes and flexing his arms repeatedly.

"Wow John is that really you!?", a girl's voice said.

"Oh it's you… uh…"

"Olivia, you forgot already?"

'I didn't even bother to learn it in the first place…', he thought to himself.

"But wow, you look so different! If it weren't for your clothes, I wouldn't have known it was you!", she said, staring at him in awe.

She began rummaging through her bag and brought out a deck of playing cards. "Do you want to play? I don't think anyone'll be here for a few minutes.", she asked while shuffling the cards.

"I-erm, I don't know how to play whatever you're playing."

"It's okay, I can teach you!"

Olivia began dealing the cards, but then the other students began flooding the classroom and filling the seats. "Or not. I guess we'll just have to wait until recess.", she said, slightly disappointed. The boy who sat in front of John turned around.

"There's no way that's you John.", said the boy.

"Who else would I be? I'm sitting here am I not?", John replied.

"Holy crap, is that you John? Hey Marcus look, it was John!", the boy responded, tugging the shirt of who John assumed was Marcus.

"Dang it Kent, everyone already knew that.", grumbled Marcus.

"Riiight, you were asking me who he was when we saw him."

"You don't gotta tell the whole world man. But dang, were you using steroids or something? You look ripped!", he exaggerated. John was still flexing his arms from anxiety, and in turn made himself look far more muscular than he really was. This was the first time John had ever had a conversation with anyone who sat around him. Normally he would have been happy, but he still felt anxious. What could possibly be causing this feeling?

A few moments later he finally understood. "Whoo! Made it just in time!". It was Dylan and his lackeys. Suddenly, the anger that laid dormant in John's body started burning once more, like oil contacting a flame. "Look at all you nerds, coming here so early. Don't you have anything better to do?", Dylan jeered. Fortunately for the class, his mocking was short-lived.

"If you plan on standing in the doorway for the entire day, then please, by all means. If not, sit down right now Dylan!", shouted Mr. Anderson. The group sat down, but not without hollering and howling with every step. Everyone else on the other hand began watching their teacher closely as he walked towards the front of the classroom. "Morning everyone! I'll be taking attendance. In the meantime why don't you tell me about how you spent your recess?"

Dylan immediately piped up. "I went to visit my cousins. It's much hotter over there than it is here. Feels like my face is freezing!", he complained. As if on cue, his lackeys began snickering loudly.

"I learned a couple magic tricks with cards. Want to see?", Olivia said, but then Mr. Anderson interrupted. "Olivia, I'm not going to take your cards, but please don't bring them out in class. You know I'll have to confiscate them if you do."

John sat in silence. He didn't want to put the spotlight on him and began lowering his head to his desk. Mr. Anderson noticed this and called out to him. "How did you spend your break, John?", he asked. John looked at his teacher and said two words before laying down on his desk.

"I exercised".

Mr. Anderson was surprised. Not by the answer, but by the fact that John had said something. In the three years he had John in his class, this was the first time he had finally managed to get John to speak in one. Mr. Anderson was about to comment on that until he stopped himself. If he were to take it the wrong way this could be his first and last time speaking in class. "Great! Are you planning on joining a team?", he asked. If he could have John talk more, maybe he would finally be comfortable with speaking in class!

"No, I just exercised.", John responded blankly.

"Really? Nothing else?", he asked, trying to keep him talking.

"No. I just exercised.", John repeated, oblivious to the fact that Mr. Anderson wanted him to keep talking.

"Ooh, ooh! Me, me!", the boy sitting next to John said, waving his hand in the air frantically. "Okay, Luke. What did you do over the break?" The boy opened his mouth, preparing to speak. The moment he did, the bell began to ring, signifying the end of homeroom. "Unfortunately, there's not enough time. Hurry along to your next class now."

Every student was dragging their feet in the halls. The break had just ended, and nobody wanted to go to class. John on the other hand rushed to the next class, but it was not because he wanted to avoid being late. The anxiety he had earlier today was gone, burned up in the flames of his anger. He needed to sit down and calm himself.

Luckily for John, today wasn't too important as far as classes went. Most of his teachers and classmates spent the classes reminiscing about what they've done during the break. John on the other hand sat silently, thinking about how glorious his vengeance would be. But beating him down wouldn't grant him the satisfaction he wanted. No, he needed to thoroughly break him in front of everyone for everything he had ever done to him to truly feel satisfied. The rest of the day passed by in the blink of an eye, up until it was time for recess.

"Hey John wait up!", Olivia said. "Let's go to the library, I did say I was going to teach you how to play!", she said mirthfully, dragging him to the school's library. As they sat down, John noticed that they were the some of the few people there. After recognizing most of the other students, he had realized something quite painful. Most of the social outcasts, everyone that was either bullied or ostracized by the rest of the school, gathered in the library during recess. Olivia, the one who dragged him to the library to play. As self-absorbed as John was, he had never seen her talk with anyone else that currently wasn't in the library nor go outside during recess. Kent and Marcus, trying as hard as they could to silently laugh in the corner. They may make everyone laugh, but they laugh at *them*, not with them. At best they were acquainted with others, but not close. A large-nosed boy with larger glasses who John thought was familiar kept staring at him eerily. There was also Luke, a thin, sickly looking boy who was always scrawling out his homework beside John every morning. *'They're all like me…'*, he thought.

John, after excusing himself from Olivia, walked towards Luke. Luke had noticed him but seemed to not pay much attention as he still had his assignments from over the break to complete.

"H-hey Luke?", said John.

Luke looked up from his papers, slightly apprehensive. "What is it, John?", he responded, voice slightly quivering in fear. Luke had his fingers around his papers, worried that John might snap once more. John noticed it but pretended he didn't. He didn't come here to yell at Luke, he didn't come to attack him or anything. "I just wanted to say I'm sorry, and thanks.", he said.

Luke stared at him as if he were an alien. What did he mean by sorry? What did he mean by thanks? Most importantly, did John of all people just apologize and thank someone, especially someone him? He was too distracted by what John had just said to comprehend that John was already leaving. As if an unknown weight he hadn't felt had finally been removed, John happily sat back down with Olivia, who was happily shuffling the cards.

The entire period passed by in the blink of an eye as he sat in the library. It wasn't mind-numbingly boring like loitering in the stairwells and corridors, it was genuinely fun! Probably the most fun John had ever had inside of a school building. When the bell rang signifying the end of recess, this was the first time John had ever been saddened by it. Kent and Marcus rushed to the door only to fall flat in front of it, tripping over each other. John and Olivia managed to stifle their laughter long enough to laugh alongside the duo once they picked themselves up from the floor. Luke seemed to want to ask John about his earlier apology but decided against it and walked towards their next class. The large nosed boy who stared at John the entire time continued to stare at him as he walked out of the library. Why? John didn't know and didn't really care to be honest.

John's spirits were high today. No longer were his emotions a sea of anger and hatred, instead they were what he could only describe as "happy". It was the first time he had ever been acquainted with anyone he knew, and if he were to be presumptuous, the first time he had ever had a friend. As if it couldn't be any better, John hadn't been ambushed by Dylan and his lackeys at all today! Just to celebrate the occasion, he shouted at the top of his lungs. "Whoo! Yeah!", he screamed on his way home. Several onlookers stared at him, but he didn't care. He was on top of the world! Just to cement the feeling, he ran a few laps around his house.

As John raced up the steps, he saw someone sitting on the corner of his bed. Smith smiled, "Someone looks happy today. I wonder if that happiness will last after you're exhausted.". John couldn't care less about his snide remarks and happily chose to begin exercising. Even after Smith was satisfied with the results, John still felt like he had endless energy despite the lack of sleep in the morning. When his parents had arrived, they were surprised by how overjoyed John was. He gobbled up his dinner, jumped around in his room, and began running around like mad. He was so excited for the next day that he could barely fall asleep, but in the end his body had reached its limit and his eyes finally closed.

John was ecstatic. Friends. *Friends*. He had friends! People he could talk with, people who understood him! In his mind, he was already thinking of countless different scenarios where he and others would go on adventures throughout the school, avoiding punishment by the skin of their teeth. John tried hard to calm himself down, he didn't want to rush things. All he did was talk with them for a bit. At best they were acquaintances, and as desperate as he may be, he couldn't really call them friends yet… but it didn't hurt to think they were!

Joy seemed to ooze out of every pore of his body, spreading to everyone around him. Though some of the other students who saw him skip and twirl happily to school would laugh at him, he didn't care.

"Oi, John! Wait up!", someone yelled.

"Oh hey Marcus!", John said happily. "Where's Kent?"

"He's part of the basketball team, so sometimes he gets to school way earlier than I do.", he replied grinning. "But what's with the skipping? Planning on taking up ballet?"

"Oh, ha-ha."

The duo hurried into the classroom, only to feel foolish remembering how early they were. Marcus jumped into his seat and began watching a video on his phone. Once John had sat down, Luke opened the door. He also rushed to his seat, but upon seeing John, he froze as if John were a snake that could strike him at any moment.

"Is something wrong?", said John. "You clearly want to ask something."

"Oh! Er, no… not really.", Luke stammered. "I was just stretching my leg…"

"Really?"

"Oh, all right I'll tell you. Y'know how yesterday you said you were sorry, and then you thanked me? What was that about? Freaked me out.", said Luke, who now regretted saying it and began bracing himself.

"That's it? Whew, I thought you were gonna ask something else! I was just saying sorry for yelling at you before the break, and thanking you for the assignments", said John, visibly trying to hold back his laughter. Luke seemed to calm down enough to finally be able to chat normally with him.

It was shaping up to be yet another great day.

Chapter 5: Anger Unleashed

Many weeks had passed since John had befriended his classmates. The violent thoughts that used to occupy his mind had left scars but had released their hold on him. He hadn't forgotten the torment that Dylan had subjected him to, but he no longer let that fury consume him. Strangely enough, Dylan also seemed to ignore John almost entirely over the last month. Maybe John's newfound strength kept him and his lackeys at bay. Maybe, which John hoped, Dylan turned over a new leaf like him and would stop bullying others… but John wouldn't hold his breath.

John woke up early in the morning as he usually did. He jogged towards the school with a grin that stretched from both ears, whistling the theme song from one of his favorite shows. John was one of the first students to come to school, beaten only by others who were a part of teams or clubs. Today however, he was the first. A few minutes later the door was suddenly opened by Olivia, who immediately dashed out upon seeing John.

"Why'd you run out like that?", John asked as soon as she walked back into the classroom, suspiciously covering her face.

"No reason! Don't mention it. Or talk about it.", she responded. She didn't face or even look in John's general direction, instead pretending to be interested in her history book. John, very clearly perturbed by this reaction, put his hand on her desk.

"Olivia, are you okay? Did something happen?", he said quietly. Olivia was the first person who had ever spoke with him that wasn't a teacher or his parents. He was NOT going to let anything happen to his friends.

"Please John… just drop it…", she whispered back.

Before John could press her further, many other students began flooding into the room. Kent and Marcus had rushed very quickly into the room, bumping into Olivia and dropping her book.

"Oh sorry Olivia, I'll get it – what happened to your?", Kent asked, but stopped once he saw Olivia glowering at him.

A few seats behind them someone snickered maliciously. John turned around to see the large-nosed boy that also went to the school library during recess who he finally recognized as one of Dylan's goons. He finally understood what had happened, or at least what he thought had happened. If that rat was laughing, that clearly means Dylan and his crew did something to Olivia. John clenched his fists, of course scum like Dylan would never change.

"I'm sorry, I shouldn't have talked with you if I knew they were going to do that.", John whispered. She turned towards John with her eyes wide in shock.

"Oh- what!?", she replied.

As John looked her face, he noticed a small bruise on her right cheek. The hatred he once had for Dylan and his friends had sprang back to life, much stronger than ever. For the first time ever, John hated Dylan on behalf of someone else. Olivia had noticed this and immediately turned around.

"This has nothing to do with them.", Olivia whispered, almost impossible to hear. "It was my m…"

However, John hadn't heard it, nor would he have heard it if she had spoken up. John had gone back to his regular routine of hating Dylan, but this time he thought his hatred was justified. The entire day he glared at him, to which seemed to throw him off which pleased John, but as far as he cared all he had done was stare at Dylan. During recess, John headed to the library, where a depressed Olivia was stacking cards. He sat down across from her, startling her and causing her to topple the house of cards. She looked incredibly flustered, muttering under her breath about how she didn't want to disturb him or how she needed to get going. John immediately grabbed her wrist and looked at her.

"Wait.", he said clearly. Strangely enough, she sat back down. "Can't you at least tell me what happened?", he asked desperately. She was the first friend he ever had; he didn't want to lose that.

"Oh you know, I got hit by a ball…", she said, not looking at him in the eyes. Suddenly he heard the snickering from earlier. The boy walked towards the duo sitting.

"It's obvious isn't it? She doesn't want to talk to a loser like you.", he said in a nasally tone. "Why else do you think she's trying to get away?"

"Who the heck are you?", John responded angrily.

"Dylan and I used to kick your butt before the break. I always thought he didn't beat you bad enough, so I always kicked you a few more times.", he answered, sneering. John had no idea who he was, Dylan always beating him up alone while one of his friends helped him.

"I don't know who you are.", John replied blankly.

"Oh I see, you're trying to diss me? Let's see if you can diss me after Dylan and I kick your butt again!", the boy said loudly to catch the attention of everyone else in the library. The boy swaggered out of the library, puffing his chest out to look larger than he actually was. Kent and Marcus, who were sitting in their usual corner, got up and walked towards John.

"Man, what a prick! He thinks he's so tough 'cause he's friends with Dylan.", Marcus replied, the annoyance on his face clear as day. "I wouldn't be surprised if that idiot was half rat. Looks the part too."

"That piece of crap's always getting Dylan to jump us. Coward can't fight his own fights.", Kent said angrily. "I bet he's in the bathroom right now washing his greasy nose. Should drown himself and do everyone a favor."

"Which bathroom?", John asked.

"The one on this floor… Hold up, you're actually going to go? Kent said, surprised.

"No, I'm going to do this alone. Make that coward learn not to mess with me. You can watch if you want, but he's mine.", John replied menacingly.

"John, no!", Olivia yelped. "If you do that, who knows what Dylan's going to do?", she begged.

"What hasn't he done? Plus I'm pretty sure he doesn't care about that loser anyway.", he replied, smirking.

John walked briskly through the halls, followed by Kent and Marcus, both of which were voicing their own grievances against the rat-faced coward. Once they had made it to the bathroom, they had locked the door. The duo were correct, he was indeed in the bathroom.

"What do you know? He *is* washing his nose!", John exclaimed.

"Oh, did you want to lick it clean for me?", the boy responded arrogantly.

"Randall's piping up huh?", Kent jeered. John began smiling wickedly. "Yeah, I don't think he knows what's about to happen.", he said, before walking menacingly towards the boy.

"You do anything to me, Dylan's going to do twice over on you.", Randall said, trying to hide his fear with smugness.

"Dylan? You have glasses for a reason. Look around, there's no Dylan for you to hide behind. Maybe if you had a cardboard cutout to hide behind?" mocked John, pretending to look around the bathroom. "But I guess you're right.", he said while lowering Randall, "You guys are just going to get me worse later…"

Randall sneered, "Good, you know your place J- ", but before he could complete his sentence, John had punched him fiercely in the face, knocking his glasses off. Kent and Marcus began cheering as John picked Randall up by the hair. "Just remembered you were the one kicking me when I was down, not Dylan.", he snarled, "I guess it's time to repay the favor!", striking him in the face once more. John began brutally kicking the boy repeatedly. Randall began coughing, but John didn't let up until his nose began bleeding.

"Oh snap! Your nose is bleeding! Gotta get that cleaned!", he mocked, dragging him across the bathroom floor by his hair. "Here, let me clean it for you!" he laughed as he began wiping the urinal with Randall's face. As soon as John let go, Randall collapsed headfirst in the urinal, crying from the pain.

"Hey John, I think he's done.", Marcus said, realizing how far John was about to take him. "Let's go."

"Go? *GO*!? You think this freaking rat left after Dylan was done kicking my butt? No, he stayed after just to get some cheap shots while I was on the ground. I'm not leaving until he's crying like a baby!", yelled John, hysterically.

Marcus was taken aback by him snapping like that. As John reminded himself of Randall's actions, the anger that had grew inside him had finally been free of its shackles. Nothing except a bloody vengeance right now would quell his rage.

"I'm sorry", Randall apologized weakly. John immediately turned towards him, "For what!? For getting checked you worthless piece of trash?!?", he said angrily before stomping on his face once more. Suddenly Kent and Marcus grabbed him and pulled him back.

"What do you think you're doing!?", John whispered angrily.

"Chill man! You're gonna kill him, calm down!", Kent exclaimed. John didn't feel like he had done enough. He was beginning to *enjoy* harming Randall… but he had released enough of his anger, enough to see reason.

"Alright, fine…", he replied, content with the beating he had just given to boy. As they began walking back to the library, the duo were whispering to each other.

"Man, John really messed that guy up… he must've really pissed him off.", Kent muttered.

"No kidding.", Marcus replied. John was too distracted to care.

John and the others had returned to the library, greeted by a depressed Olivia, and a confused Luke. He stared at John as if he had never seen him in his life and Olivia couldn't bear to face him at all. As soon as John sat down, Kent and Marcus began applauding silently. "Man you should have seen what he did to Randall!", Kent marveled. "I know right? Never knew you knew how to fight John. Got that little turd good!", Marcus nodded in appreciation. Luke on the other hand was terrified.

"John, getting into a fight?", Luke muttered to himself.

"Aww come on Luke, Randall didn't stand a chance. It was a beatdown.", laughed Kent. "Plus the little turd had it coming! He pisses everyone off. Nobody'll know who did that to him.", Marcus added.

"Oh, John you shouldn't have…", Olivia said. "Neither should you two have either… what if you get into trouble?". The duo laughed in response.

"So what?", Kent asked. "Everyone's always beating each other up, it's nothing new."

The library door opened, revealing a bruised and battered Randall clutching his glasses. A distinct stench of urine and soap followed him. His eyes were bloodshot from crying, body shuddering with rage, and a limp that showed his pain.

"Don't th-think you're g-getting away with this…", he stuttered angrily. As if Randall's words flicked a switch, John smirked maliciously.

"Or what? Gonna get sic your dog on me? What's going to stop me from getting you when Dylan's not around?", he asked. John began snickering. He then glanced at his friends thinking what he did was pretty cool, but it seemed like they didn't think so. Kent and Marcus exchanged looks with each other, eyebrows raised slightly showing the slightest hint of surprise. Olivia's frown almost completely disappeared, but the concern was still there, and Luke was slowly shifting his seat away from him..

Randall limped away as the bell rang, and everyone else followed him out. A strange feeling passed through John, almost euphoric. He had hurt someone, and the elation he felt clouded his thoughts. He couldn't care less about what the people he considered friends thought. His hatred for Dylan wasn't gone, but he finally understood the kind of joy one could derive from the suffering of others. A kind of taboo happiness only enjoyed by the people with power, and John enjoyed every moment of it.

Chapter 6: John's Brutality

On the following day, John had woken up much later than usual. He was almost certainly late for class. '*Who cares? There's a billion and a half people late every day, one more won't make a difference*', he thought to himself. Today he needed to stand out. What he once considered stupid and unimportant now became

The closer he walked towards the school, the more students he saw. Most of the students that had noticed him were quite shocked by how much he had changed. John had expected this. In fact, he wanted this reaction. He needed to show the riffraff he was no longer a part of them. From all of the attention he was now receiving, the grin on his face stretched further. Even though he didn't plan it, it still worked out in his favor as more kids seemed to watch him. '*If they thought that was surprising, wait till they see this!*', he thought as he noticed a certain person walking meekly towards the school.

"What's going on, Rat-Face?", John said, grabbing Randall by the back of his collar. Randall made a loud squeaking noise in terror.

"O-oh hey John! Didn't think you'd be so late to class…", the boy said, trembling.

"Yeah, I didn't think so either, but I gotta make myself look good, ya know?", John replied, sneering. "By the way, I vaguely recall you saying some stuff about how I "wasn't going to get away with this."". By now, many students were watching. Randall began whispering, "You don't got the balls to start anything here…". The boy's voice was shaking with fear but had a hint of his usual smugness. He knew there would be no way that John could ever get away with beating him down, especially if he were to do so as brutally as yesterday.

John whispered back to the frightened boy, "You think I don't? If you want me to kick your butt, I'll do it for you right now!", he said, Shoving Randall onto the floor. The boy laid there for a second, as if he didn't expect John to follow through with his threat. Once he tried to get up, John punted him from behind launching him even further. Before the boy could get up once more, John had put his foot down on his back.

"I'm sorry! Please, I'm sorry, I won't bother you ever again!", Randall pleaded, tears beginning to form around his eyes.

John had a wicked sneer across his face. He surveyed the area and waited a moment until the few students who were watching had ran off. He raised his foot and stared at the small boy, who immediately took the opportunity to scurry away. It didn't matter though. He already got what he wanted, harming Randall was just an added benefit.

Though it may have seemed odd to the students, who were now both surprised and horrified by what they had just witnessed, John had carefully planned this out. Randall was thoroughly terrified, and the other students would have spread rumors throughout the halls. At the end of the day, they were just rumors with no real weight, but should they see Randall scurry away at the sight of John, the rumors would become fact in their eyes. By the time he had gotten into the school, the next period had started, and everyone was flooding out of their classrooms to get to their next class… but not before they caught a quick glimpse of John strutting through the halls.

Unfortunately, John didn't think their reactions were appropriate enough. Over the next few days John's brutality had been steadily increasing and his attire had undergone massive changes to match. The messy black hair was now brushed back, the bland inoffensive clothing now replaced by vivid colors that were harsh on the eyes. Glaring at the other students also worked at unnerving them. Such a drastic change over the course of a few days would surely get the attention of everyone else… but that wasn't the only thing he was after. What he wanted was revenge, and he knew exactly how to get it.

John rarely visited the library with his friends anymore. Instead, he would go outside with the other students looking for new targets. All of his aggression was focused on a single group, people he despised. He began hunting them like an animal, waiting for them to separate from their groups and out of the sight of prying eyes. If he couldn't do that, he'd verbally harass them instead. As his arrogance grew, so too did the circle of his targets.

John did not care whatsoever if any members of the staff caught him. Excluding Mr. Anderson, they cared about John's reign of terror as much as John cared about being merciful. His viciousness hadn't gone unnoticed, however. The members of Dylan's group began giving John a wide berth as to not incur his wrath. The other students no longer walked around him at all. But worst of all, the people he considered friends had distanced themselves from John. Oddly enough, John felt uneasy and decided to confront them.

John opened the library door and slammed it loudly before strutting towards the area where his friends usually gathered. Everyone around him immediately turned their face towards him. Luke began nudging his chair away from John's table slightly. Olivia didn't have the same concerned face as before, but as if she were trying to read him. Kent and Marcus were leering at him as if they didn't know who he was.

"Man, what's wrong with you guys?", said John.

"Haha, you know, little bit of this and that…", Kent replied faintly. It was obvious from his voice he definitely didn't want to talk, or rather, he was trying to distance himself from John.

John quickly began feeling a sense of desperation building inside of him and tried to start up some small talk, "You know that annoying kid that's always yelling after every class? I cornered him last period in the bathroom. Was pretty funny how he squealed like a pig every time I punched him haha!"

Olivia glared at him, "You beat him up… because he annoyed you?", she asked.

"Uh, yeah?", responded John, mildly concerned by that reaction. Normally when Dylan laughed about how he beat up others with his lackeys, they laughed alongside him. He looked towards the others, looking to see their reactions.

"Hey Kent, you saw Randall anywhere? I've been looking for him for a while now."

"I don't think you would since you embarrassed him in front of the entire school. That was pretty messed up."

"H-hey man, didn't you say that little rat deserved it? With how he hides behind people bigger than him and all that?".

But then Marcus interjected, "Yeah, but what about everyone else? Are you out of your god damn mind? You should be grateful nobody's going to punish you for that!", he responded angrily. "Randall may have gotten what was coming to him, but what the heck is all that crap with beating up people who did absolutely nothing to you?", Upon hearing this, John laughed halfheartedly.

"Don't worry. Dylan's been doing much worse, and he never even gotten detention or anything."

"Come on… I thought you guys would understand… You're my friends, right?", he said, his voice getting fainter by the second.

"'I thought you guys would understand'. What the heck is wrong with you!?", Olivia responded angrily. "I understood why you felt the need to get revenge on Randall. I might not have liked it, but I understood! But the others did nothing to you!"

John sat there, stunned in disbelief. "Wh-what!? I beat him up 'cause Randall hurt you! I thought YOU of all people would have understood why I did it!"

"No! no he didn't. I told you it had nothing to do with that! Do you think I want to talk about how my mom abuses me!? You think you're some kind of superhero beating up bad guys for some damsel in distress?", she interrupted, the contempt visible on her face clearer than before. "And what about the others? They did absolutely nothing, and yet you still jumped them!"

"B-but what about what he said!?"

"What about it!? Everyone knows Randall is a jerk!"

"You didn't have a problem that day! A few days ago you were worried about ME!"

"And I was wrong to do so. You're just as much of a jerk like the rest of those bullies who think they're above everyone else. I can't believe you did all that! It's almost as if you *wanted* to get into trouble!"

John's eyes were bulging with anger. He had half a mind to smack Olivia across the face.

"Listen, John. Randall's just like that. He likes riling people up. Nobody likes him, that's why Marcus and I – ", said Kent.

"You shut up! Why are you complaining? You even said he deserved it! You came with me when I first beat Randall up-"

"Stop shouting! Yeah, we did say that, and yeah we did go with you. But then you started beating up random people for no freaking reason!", Marcus shouted back.

"I TOLD you! We aren't going to get in trouble!"

"That is not the point you idiot!"

John was absolutely livid, but he left them in silence. He had half a mind to get up and start smashing them with the chair he sat on, but he walked out, thinking about what they all just said. He thought they were his friends, but they had betrayed him! Their words stung as if they had each just stabbed him in the back. A few weeks ago, John would have been broken by that, but not this time. His arrogance had planted an idea, and this recent betrayal had nurtured the seed. This would just be the beginning.

The end of the day was rapidly approaching. Everyone was restless in homeroom, but they were all thinking of the same thing, about John. He had been on a rampage for a few days and the news spread like wildfire but none of them had actually seen it happen. Most of them couldn't believe the once meek John who hung around the other nerds in the library could be a violent psychopath. However none of the students bothered telling any authority figures. Dylan had been on a rampage since he had ever set foot in the school and he had never gotten so much as a detention. They knew John would be treated the same. All they could do is lay low and weather the storm.

"John", Mr. Anderson said. He didn't need to say more. His face said the rest. He wanted to talk to John once everyone had left. As the students began flooding out of the class, John stayed behind.

"John. Why did you do it?", he asked.

"Do what?"

"You know what I'm talking about."

John began to smile. "Are you talking about the rumors about me? They're rumors. They aren't real.", he lied.

"John, why? Surely someone like you who was bullied would understand what kind of pain you had caused?"

"I don't know what you are talking about. And even if I did understand, so? There's an entire cabal of bullies going around harassing the students, and *nothing* is done to them. I don't see you lecturing them about what they're doing, and yet here you are lecturing me over some stupid rumors!"

Mr. Anderson closed his eyes. John's responses were sadly correct. The rest of the staff were incompetent or corrupt buffoons living paycheck to paycheck, the dean even more so. It was the same with Dylan. The school doesn't even attempt to punish wrongdoers; in their inaction, it incentivized wrongdoing. There wasn't an acceptable answer to give, and John knew that.

Terrifying Dylan's lackeys fueled his arrogance, increasing his scope of targets to people who have done nothing to him, but in his eyes, they were people who stood by and did nothing while he was at Dylan's mercy. He no longer needed friends, the company of other losers and conformists meant nothing to him. As for Mr. Anderson? He was just a teacher. The only teacher who cared, but unlike his lazy and incompetent peers and superiors, he didn't have the power to punish John in any meaningful way. John had become so notoriously violent among the other students that his presence was enough for them to leave. His viciousness didn't stop at the school walls either. He had begun to treat his parents with disdain, to which his father thought was just a phase. Playing games no longer occurred to him, he now had access to something that offered him much more entertainment that a game could ever provide.

John had finally gotten what he had always dreamed of. To finally rise up against those who oppressed him. To finally feel like he was on the top. To finally understand how it felt on stepping on those beneath him. And once he had tasted this delicious, forbidden nectar, he was never going to forget it.

Chapter 7: Nightmares

'But what's wrong? Why do I still feel like dirt?', John thought to himself. Twenty pushups, thirty, forty… he stopped caring about the amount. All he wanted was to exhaust himself, to be too tired to be caught up in his emotions. Why? *Why*? Why did he still feel like something was "missing"?

"Feels terrible, doesn't it?", said a voice he hadn't heard in ages.

"Wha- Smith is that you?", John said aloud. Smith hadn't appeared before him in quite a long time. However, something was different, something nobody would have noticed unless they saw it repeatedly. The arrogant and knowing sneer that he appeared with wasn't there. Instead, Smith's face had the look of someone who had been thoroughly broken.

"What do you mean?", John asked. "I've finally been able to get my revenge on nearly everyone who had ever pissed me off! Why the heck would you care!? Didn't you say I needed to stand up for myself? That's exactly what I did!"

Smith shook his head. "True, you *did* stand up for yourself. And? What of it? You've gotten nearly everything you've ever wanted. And yet… you still feel terrible."

John was at a loss of words. True, he did finally get his revenge, or most of it. True, he was no longer a spiteful weakling, or not as much as he used to be. True, he managed to change… but something was missing! What was it? It was on the tip of his tongue, much like ninety percent of the synonyms he could have used when speaking and writing to sound more intelligent or to pad on extra length to assignments. He couldn't find the answer! John looked towards Smith for an answer, but instead of an answer, he turned away and disappeared without a word.

That night, John fell ill. The stress of not knowing what was missing was eating at him. His skin felt cold and heavy, his tongue drier than a desert. Three times he rose from his bed, dragging himself into the bathroom to throw up. Was he dying? He made a silent prayer, hoping that he wasn't. He got up once more to empty out what remained in his stomach.

"John… Are you okay?", a worried voice said behind him.

"Yeah, just don't feel so good.", he muttered before retching once more.

"If you don't feel better in the morning, you can stay home if you'd like. If you need water, I'll bring it to your room… just don't push yourself too hard…", said his father.

John lumbered back to his room. His skin felt so sensitive that even the slightest brush against the walls was like rubbing a cold knife over his skin. Time seemed to slow down with every movement and the hallway felt as if it was extending by two paces for every one he took. By the time he had made it to his room, the clock on his dresser read half past four. After drinking the water with as much care as possible, he slowly slipped into bed, hoping that maybe he would wake up feeling much better.

How wrong he was.

"Open your eyes kid, or I'll open them for you.", a voice ordered.

"Uh? Morning already? I just fell asleep!", John thought. His eyelids felt much heavier than usual, as if they didn't want to be raised. He put his strangely wet hands onto his face to open his eyelids for him. Once he finally managed to raise them, he wished he hadn't. Bones scattered about, flesh and organs splattered everywhere, decapitated and dismembered bodies, flayed corpses, all either floating grotesquely in an ankle-deep pool of blood or packed together like disgusting flesh islands. It was a vision of utmost horror, and yet despite being horrified, John felt a sense of belonging.

"Am I dead? Is this Hell?", John thought. *"Wait what? Why am I hearing my voice in my head when I talk?"*

"*You aren't dead*", a voice said behind him. John immediately turned to face the voice and saw Smith standing in the pool of blood. "*At least, not yet anyway.*"

"*As for where you are? Isn't that obvious?*"

"*Yes, very obvious!*", said John sarcastically. "*Some sort of pit of death and despair! I come here every single day.*"

"*You got that right. You DO come here every single day, to this pit of death and despair.*", said Smith, sneering at John.

"*I was being sarcastic.*"

"*I wasn't.*"

John was taken aback by that response. He didn't know of any bloody pits filled with corpses, blood, and organs. Even if he did, it's not like he would make it a habit to return there every single day. He began wading through the blood, seeing if he could find something, anything. The blood pool seemed to get deeper throughout the middle, he didn't want to swim, but there was a small "island" of flesh and bone across it. He swam across the pool of blood until he reached the shore of the island. This island was similar to the one where John woke up. The only difference was a grotesque, hill shaped monument of sorts of the corpse of a small child strung up, arms chained to a metal rod, holding a large, sharp blade in place.

"Where the heck am I!?", he thought. John looked in every direction. All he could see was an ocean of blood, littered with small islands of flesh, bone, and corpses. He was beginning to panic, what if there *wasn't* a way out of here? What if he had been brought here to die?

COUGH COUGH

John immediately turned around, terrified. He turned to face the monument, which turned out to be a dying child who had his skin flayed and was left chained here to bleed to death.

"Are you alright? What happened here?", John asked, horrified. The boy raised his head, flesh and skull visible. A sight which would have terrified anyone including John… but strangely, it made him excited?

"I'm sorry! Please, I'm sorry, I won't bother you ever again!.", the dying child pleaded in a raspy, dying voice. John was horrified, who could have possibly done something like this? …But the words sounded familiar, as if John had heard them very recently.

"I'm sorry! Please, I'm sorry, I won't bother you ever again!.", the dying child pleaded once more.

"Okay, just… calm down. Can you tell me who did this to you?", John asked.

"I'm sorry! Please, I'm sorry, I won't bother you ever again!."

"Yes, you said that already, now can you calm down please. Who did this to you?"

"I'm sorry! Please, I'm sorry, I won't bother you ever again!."

The boy wasn't right in the head, he must have lost his sanity ages ago… but it was something about what he was saying. John *knew* he had heard it somewhere, but *where*? Where could he have heard someone plead like this?

"I'm sorry! Please, I'm sorry, I won't bother you ever again!."

"I'm sorry! Please, I'm sorry, I won't bother you ever again!."

"I'm sorry! Please, I'm sorry, I won't bother you ever again!."

"I'm sorry! Please, I'm sorry, I won't bother you ever again!."

"Plea- ", but then John interrupted. *"SHUT UP ALREADY! This is the tenth time you've said it already!"*

"-se, stop! I'm sorry, please. I won't do it again."

'*Wait,* **ten** *times? Why did I say ten? That was the ninth time he said it…* ', John thought to himself. He realized he did in fact here it somewhere. His eyes turned back towards the dying boy… but the boy began to change before his very eyes! First his skin, then clothing began forming, and then his face.

"I'm sorry! Please, I'm sorry, I won't bother you ever again!.", said Randall. John's hatred flared as soon as he saw Randall's face. As soon as it did, a large fleshy body formed behind the metal rod and smashed the chain holding the blade in place. The large blade now loose began plummeting.

"Please, stop! I'm sorry, pl- ", Randall began to say.

SPLAT

The sickening sound of the blade slicing straight through Randall's flesh and cutting him in half seemed to echo throughout the area. As soon as Randall's body was sliced in half, the skin and clothes seemed to disintegrate until he looked just like the boy who had been chained there earlier. John stood there for what seemed like an eternity to him, stunned by what he had just witnessed.

'What IS *this place!?",* John thought to himself. His entire body was shaking in fear. He had been afraid before, but never to this degree. Why was this happening? Was this his punishment for attacking others? Who was doing this to him? How did they do this? He was alone here in this lake of blood. Not a single soul around to help him… but something felt odd! As disgusted as he were by the piles of flesh and

corpses, as horrified as he were by the 'death' of Randall… there was a feeling inside him he couldn't describe. Or maybe it was a feeling he knew but didn't want to admit.

As John stood there in shock, he saw another island that was larger than the one he was currently standing on. He could feel it calling to him, but he was still paralyzed by fear, he didn't want to move… but then his body started moving! John tried all he could to stay in place, but his body refused to take any orders.

"No! Stop! Don't go there!", he screamed, but his body kept swimming through the blood.

The second island was very large but unlike the previous one, a giant pit took up a majority of it. He peered into it, but it was pitch black. Whatever could be in a hole this deep, he didn't want to know, and he was sure he didn't want to stand around such a giant hole anyway.

"Know what this is?", Smith asked, appearing right behind John.

"Holy crap! You scared me, almost knocked me into that hole!", John yelled.

John didn't get to finish saying what he wanted. As soon as Smith appeared, a sound started coming from the pit. The sound of dozens of people crying, screaming, yelling, shouting. They all blended together to form a loud ghastly wailing as it rose up to the exit. Every single hair on John's body stood up.

"Wh-what is that!?", said John, in a much higher-pitched voice than usual.

"You still haven't figured out what this place is? I'm surprised!"

"Why would I know about this place? How many places do I know that looks like this!?"

"Think John, think!", he commanded, tapping on his temple. *"You of all people should know this place, and how dreadful it is."*

*"Well I **don't** know what this place is, and even if I did, how the heck would YOU know!?"*

Smith began laughing loudly. *"Oh I bet you'd like to know do you? I bet you'd like to know why I know your deepest secrets, why I know so much about you?"*

"I JUST SAID I DO. ARGH! YOU AREN'T HELPING ME AT ALL! WHY ARE YOU EVEN HERE!?"

John stormed off into the other direction. Conveniently, he managed to spot yet another island, this one much larger than the previous two. Whatever forced his body to the other island wasn't helping him here, maybe it knew he wanted to get to the next island. Either way John had to swim, and swim he did all the while cursing Smith in his thoughts. The blood around him seemed to feel warmer the angrier he got, but John paid no mind. It felt much better than earlier.

This third island was very strange compared to the previous two. There was no pit, no corpses excluding the ones that the island was composed of. Instead, it had one giant wall of flesh, wide enough to hide an entire building behind it and tall enough that he couldn't see the top of it. Regardless, there was nothing to see or do on this island nor was there any way to escape this, wherever he was.

"What now? There's nothing else here. No exit, no nothing.", said John loudly. *"Smith! What is this place!?"*

"You still haven't figured it out? Hmm, no. You know where this is, you just don't want to believe it.", said Smith, appearing immediately after being called.

"So what is this place then?"

Smith's eyes narrowed, *"You know this place. Think fool, think! What use is your brain if you do not know how to use it!?"*

"I'm thinking! I've never been to a place like this!", John shouted angrily.

"How long are you going to drag your feet? If I know what this place is, then you know!"

"I JUST TOLD YOU I DON'T! HOW WOULD I KNOW WHAT THIS PLACE IS!?"

"I won't tell you anything. Have fun.", said Smith, disappearing once more.

"SMITH, GOD DAMN IT, JUST TELL ME! Come back!", yelled John. *"Now I'm stuck here, stupid wall in my way."*, he said as he kicked the wall. To John's surprise, the wall began parting but he wish it hadn't. Behind the wall were multiple pillories, each holding a person, and a mound of flesh, bone, and assorted body parts piled behind them. There was someone else there with John. It was… John? The other John was holding a large axe and covered head to toe in a dark garb that was splattered with flesh and blood.

"I always thought he didn't beat you bad enough, so I always kicked you a few more times.", the hooded John began saying. As soon as the other John finished talking he slammed his axe into the body, splattering pieces of flesh everywhere. It then threw the remaining bits into the pile of flesh behind it.

"Aww, what's the rush? You didn't even say 'bye'!", the hooded John asked the corpse beside the first one. It too was crushed by the

axe. One by one the other John spoke to the corpses. One by one they were crushed into tiny pieces. One by one they began reforming and the hooded John continued to talk. Whether it was fear or amazement, John stood there wide-eyed and silent. The corpses kept stacking onto the mound until it began spilling into the bloody sea surrounding the island.

"Where the heck do you think you're going, punk?", the hooded John bellowed, grabbing another body lying on the ground. As he did, the body began transforming to look like Dylan. A horribly sickening thought crossed his mind once he knew what was about to happen.

"No... NO!", John shouted. The hooded began crushing the body of Dylan with the weight of the axe, repeating the same taunts and insults Dylan used to say when he was crushing John.

"Now do you get it? You know what this place is, you just couldn't bring yourself to believe it.", said Smith, appearing once more.

"Is this... my imagination?", whispered John, horrified by the realization.

"Your mind..."

"So when you meant – "

"Exactly. Every single day when you're thinking about how you're going to exact your revenge on every single person who wronged you in the slightest, this is how your mind looks."

"Oh my God..."

"You've spent your entire life obsessed with revenge on everyone who wronged you in the slightest. Look at this place! Have you ever given a single thought about what you'll do after *you get your revenge?"*

"Are you trying to tell me to give up on getting back at them? I can't just change can I? It's not like I have any other choice..."

"But you CAN!", Smith responded angrily. *"And you DID! When you pushed your body to the limit, you didn't think about killing everyone that wronged you. When you were surrounded by your friends, you had forgotten about the torment you were subjected to."*

"I couldn't care less whether or not you got your vengeance. What matters is what you're going to do afterwards. You had found a place where you were wanted, but then you threw that away for all this hate you've pent up inside yourself!", ranted Smith.

"Fine. I did. But I burned those bridges. It's not like I can just go to them and say, "Sorry for everything I did, can we go back to normal?"", said John.

"Who said you can't?"

"I did. What I did was the equivalent of spitting in their mouths. I can't just go back and apologize."

"Why do you assume they want you to apologize? They are your friends. They invited you to their circle for a reason, they saw something in you that they saw in themselves.", said Smith.

Smith's words sank into John's mind, almost literally. As they did, another feeling washed over him. Remorse. His past actions sickened him. He never wanted to be like Dylan, tormenting and harassing countless students. He never wanted to *like* hurting others. He just wanted to be himself, but he spent far too long seething with rage. It was time to move on.

John woke up before dawn that morning. Though the finer details of that nightmare were difficult to remember, it had etched a message in his mind. His sickness from the other day was gone, now left with an aching reminder within his body.

Chapter 8: Doubts and Concerns

"It'll be fun! Better than sitting inside all day anyway!", John's father said.

"I don't know anything about fishing. I don't see how this would be fun."

"Don't be like that, John. Your father and I also don't know anything about fishing.", his mother chided.

"Then why are we going fishing if none of us know how?", asked John.

"Don't worry. I'm sure we'll figure it out soon enough. I brought a guide with me!"

John sat in the back seat, groaning and grumbling about all the time he could have spent playing games. Instead, his parents decided to go fishing, something none of them knew how to do.

"And… we're here! John help me get everything out, will you?"

"Fine, it'll probably be the most interesting thing I'll do while we're here…", he grumbled.

As John helped his father get everything ready, he noticed how different everything felt from yesterday. The cool air, the sun beaming down on him, the lack of noise. It would have been perfect were it not for the fact that John didn't bring anything with him to pass the time.

"Now if I'm reading this correctly, we need to do – ", his father grunted as he tried to attach the bait to the hook while also trying to read the guidebook he brought along with him. "-this! And we should be good to go!"

The hook sailed through the air before it landed into the water with a satisfying "plop".

"And now, we wait.", his father said, before adjusting himself to relax in his chair.

John sat beside his father, bored out of his mind. There was absolutely nothing to do. No games, no books, nothing to pass the time.

"Did anything happen?", his father said suddenly.

"Wha- oh no… not really."

"One day, when you get older and have kids of your own, you'll realize that we were also young once. We can usually tell when you're hiding something."

John sat there silently. His father was right, he did have something to say. Strangely, he couldn't work up the courage to say it. Instead, John waited for the perfect opportunity to say what was on his mind. A way to slip it in quietly while his parents were occupied with other things, or maybe when he could quietly combine it with something else to talk about. It wasn't something he was confident in that he could just blurt out randomly.

Unfortunately for John, he wasn't accustomed to long periods of doing nothing that didn't involve sleeping. There was only so much cloud watching he could handle without going mad.

"…ad? Dad?", croaked John.

"Hmm?"

"Let's just say something happened and I… something happened and now… something happened."

"That's an awful lot of 'something happened'!", exclaimed his father. "Have you tried apologizing? If this 'something happened' because of you, then try apologizing. You might not go back to how things were before, but a sincere apology will help you feel better."

"John… you, you aren't getting bullied are you?", his mother asked.

"What? No!"

"Oh I knew it! I'm going to call the school once we get back. I can't believe I didn't see it earlier, oh my – ", cried his mother.

"I am NOT getting bullied."

"Then what's wrong!? You haven't told us anything other than 'something happened'!"

"Nothing happened! Never mind.", grumbled John, regretting talking about anything now. He had forgotten how worried his mother would get whenever he had something he needed to say.

"We've been sitting here forever, and yet nothing. What a waste of time…", mumbled John.

"Not quite. You managed to get something off your chest didn't you?", said his father. "Who cares if we didn't catch anything?"

As his father reeled in the lines, John caught a glimpse of the hooks. None of them were baited! This entire outing must have been a way for his parents to find out what was on his mind. Truthfully, he was grateful that his parents did something like this for him, but he was still slightly peeved that it ate into his free time.

As John got home, he immediately jumped onto his computer and immediately started playing what used to be the game he spent most of his time on.

As soon as he logged in, he was immediately bombarded with messages from his friends.

"Wait, the knight actually logged in!", said the mage. *"Didn't I tell you? People like us can't spend so much time with normal people that long. He was going to come back sooner or later."*

"Where have you been!? You haven't played for a month!", the ranger asked.

"Yeah, I was busy with some in-real-life stuff, I wasn't able to play. Sorry guys.", John responded. *"What did I miss?"*

"Only a whole new continent and all. Speaking of which, you're pretty far behind. I can lend you some equipment, but you'll need to catch up if we want to group up again.", the ranger replied. *"It's pretty hard trying to do things alone. Most people are already part of groups."*

"Well then, I guess I'll do some catching up."

"So how are things? You've been gone for a while."

"Oh nothing much, just some stuff with friends and family."

"See! I told you he became normal!", the ranger exclaimed. *"I told you we would need a replacement!"*

"No he didn't. If he did he wouldn't be playing this game anymore.", said the mage. *"Either that or he's no longer normal, but it's not like we should hate him for that. He's just lucky he got out."*

"What? Didn't you say how happy you were when you were working from home?"

"Nah man, it was nice for a few days. Then I realized the only human contact I had was at the office. I've stopped working from home a few days ago.", the mage responded. *"You'll see in a few weeks."*

"Thanks mage, you mind if I ask you a question?", asked John,

"Sure, go for it. But I might not have the answer."

"Let's say some stuff happened between me and a few others. What could I do to, say, apologize for what I did?"

"That depends on…", pondered the mage. *"Why do you want to apologize? Do you want to apologize, or do you need to apologize?"*

"What's the difference?", asked John,

"Are they really your friends? Or are they just a part of whatever clique you're in and they're pressuring you?"

"I don't know… what are you saying?"

"He's asking if they're really your friends or just some idiots taking advantage of you. You can't trust normal people, and besides, they'll probably forget what happened in a week or two.", the ranger responded.

"I know a friendless loser like me shouldn't be giving relationship advice, but you shouldn't apologize unless you did something truly abhorrent. Ranger may be crass, but he's not far off.", the mage said. *"If they really were your friends, then they've already forgiven you. It's just you holding yourself back. Nobody who deserves an apology* asks *for one, nor do they expect it."*

John logged off shortly after. Maybe now he was ready to finally face the people he once called friends.

Chapter 9: Expectations and Reality

It had been a while since John was terrified of going to school. This time it wasn't the fear of assault that terrified him, it was the response he would receive from his friends. The weight seemed to crush him and every step towards the school made his body heavier and heavier.

'Why not just try tomorrow?'', he thought. The closer he got to the school, the louder the thought got.

'And if I don't have the courage tomorrow, I could always wait until the day after tomorrow…'. The thought was beginning to grow like a small parasitic plant. Every step he took towards the school made it grow faster and faster until he finally stopped moving. The weight of his body and mind finally got the better of him and stopped him from moving any further. It was the worst feeling ever. An icy feeling crept down his back making his hairs stand up on end. An odd sensation like nausea, but not quite, made his vision a bit shaky. His entire mouth was drier than a desert despite the cool weather. Was it fear? Was he afraid of what might happen if he tried to make amends? Either way, he wasn't moving any closer to school. John stood there silently for what seemed like an eternity in his mind.

Finally, he had made his decision. John sprinted towards the school as fast as he could… but he avoided speaking with anyone. All the preparation he made to steel himself broke down like a sandcastle against the waves of reality. It had been quite a long time since he wished for classes to end sooner. It had been a while since he stalked the halls during recess to avoid everyone. It had been far too long, but it was his punishment for not facing his friends.

"Hey, JOHN!", hollered Marcus.

John froze in his tracks and turned his head slightly to see Kent and Marcus beckoning him closer. Instead, he sprinted off in the opposite direction. He didn't know why he ran; it was an unconscious reaction. By the time he was done running, he found himself in the bathroom halfway across the school.

"Man, they'll be really pissed now", he thought. Maybe he'll wait a week until they forget, or a month! Maybe next year. Or maybe he could wait until after they graduate. Maybe he could just avoid them forever. That'd be easier than whatever he was afraid of.

"Or maybe you should stop losing your nerve and face them you pathetic coward!", a thought sprung in his mind.

John knew he needed to reconcile with his friends, but actually following through with that pressured him as if he were thousands of feet underwater.

"I'm going to do it!", he thought, looking at the exit of the bathroom.

"Any moment now, I'll go…", but he didn't budge an inch from where he stood.

"Okay, on three…"

"One…"

"Two…"

"… Two and a half…"

"Two and three quarters.", but then his thoughts were interrupted by another student entering the bathroom. The student wasn't there for John nor did he care about why John was standing there like a statue, but that's not what he thought.

"AAAAAAAAAAAAAAGH!", John screamed at the top of his lungs before bolting out of the bathroom. His mind was tearing itself apart. He wanted to reconcile with his friends, but what if they didn't? What if the only people who had accepted him turned their backs on him? What then? As he walked towards his classroom, his mind was warring with itself.

"I worked out for months to be strong enough to get my revenge on Dylan. Why am I worried about something that'll take a minute to do?"

"I worked out because I hated him and had nothing to lose if I did so. If I fail at getting back with the others, I'll be all alone again."

"But I'm alone right now! *If I don't do anything, or they reject me, nothing will have changed!"*

"But what if they do reject me? What if waiting a week or two could have changed the result? Being alone for a while would be the same as before I befriended them. I could wait out a week or two…"

"And what if the result doesn't change? I'd just be torturing myself for absolutely no reason at all."

"But what if it did change? I'd just be shooting myself in the foot right now!"

"Better to get over it now than beat myself up for a week."

"Yeah, I'd just beat myself up over it for the rest of my life instead."

Distracted by his own thoughts, John wasn't paying attention to anything around him. Once John got to class, he didn't notice Olivia whispering his name, he couldn't see Kent trying to get his attention. He was stuck in battle with his own mind.

"They're right in front of me right now! Nothing's stopping me from apologizing, or even trying to talk to them!"

"Remember what happened the last time I apologized to someone? Luke thought I was dying or something!"

"Yeah, but then he understood after I explained why I apologized."

"After a week! After a week of avoiding me. It'll just be worse if I do anything now. Besides, it'll probably be easier to talk with them one at a time instead of right now. The pressure would kill me!"

"So I'm just going to sit here in silence like before? I'm back at square one!"

"I don't have any other choice do I?"

So he sat there uncomfortably. Trying to avoid looking at anyone else, going back to his old habit of laying down on his desk pretending to sleep. John hated it, but what else could he do? The others around him exchanged glances with one another. John was behaving stranger than he normally did. Something was clearly wrong with him.

Dylan too was watching John. Not as intently as the people surrounding John but stealing looks every so often. John was one of the victims of his bullying, except unlike the other suckers, he was the first to actually fight back. Today, John wasn't oozing the confidence he normally did. He didn't attack any of his cronies either nor did he try to intimidate them. It wasn't as if Dylan was *scared* of him nor was he afraid of getting beaten by him. Tormenting someone he saw as beneath him shouldn't take effort.

John rushed home after school faster than he had ever done. The second he got home, he jumped up the stairs into his room, pulling his hair and flailing about in anger.

"Stupid, stupid, stupid! I should have just talked with them argh! What am I even DOING!?", he wailed.

"See? I should have just spoken with them!"

"I'd be feeling even worse if I did though!"

"No I wouldn't! Nothing could be worse than this!"

"It'd feel way worse knowing I've lost all my friends."

"I've been alone before. I could handle that. What I can't handle is this torment every single day! That's why I pushed myself to become stronger than Dylan was! And look, now he hasn't bothered me since winter recess!"

John couldn't handle his mind ripping itself apart by his indecisiveness. The only way he knew how to stop it was to exhaust himself to the point where he could no longer think. After struggling through his homework with what little space in his head he had that wasn't occupied, he began exerting himself. Hopefully, it would work, and he'd finally be able to relax.

"Maybe I should skip classes tomorrow and work things out.", he thought while running up and down the stairs.

"THIRTY-ONE!", he said through gritted teeth to distract himself from his thoughts.

"And what if they think I'm avoiding them because I'm too cool to hang around them? If I skip tomorrow, it'd make that theory sound even more reasonable."

"Beats going to school and ignoring them in their face."

"FORTY-THREE!", said John in the middle of his sit-ups.

"So instead of ignoring them, I'll just talk to them. It's NOT that hard. In fact, trying to ignore them is HARDER than just talking with them."

"If that were the case, I wouldn't freeze up or run away whenever they were near me."

"And it'll only get worse if I don't talk to them! If I get this over with now, then I won't have to suffer like this!"

"FIFTY- ", he said before his hand slipped in the middle of a pushup. As soon as he hit the ground he began pounding the floor in a fit of rage, tired in both body and mind and worse off than he was before. If he had just spoken with his friends none of this would have happened, but he was too socially incompetent to do that.

John laid there on the floor, defeated. His body tired, his mind even more so. Tears flowed down his face like a waterfall. He deserved this for everything he had done. Suffering alone was the only way he could atone for what he had done to everyone around him.

'Why can't I have just been normal? Why me?', thought John. Feeling nothing but despair, he dragged his tired body and laid on his bed, crying himself to sleep.

Chapter 10: Futility

Messy hair, bland inoffensive clothing, dull eyes, trudging along like someone who was tired of life itself… John had almost completely reverted to how he was in the beginning of the school year with the slight difference of his now pronounced musculature. He was like a walking corpse among the sea of students flooding into the school.

"What d'you think's going on with him?", Kent asked Marcus, pointing at John shambling about. "He looks like he's sleepwalking."

"I dunno man. He was always pretty weird though wasn't he?", responded Marcus.

"Yeah, but he looks like a zombie."

"It's not like we can ask him what's going on. Every time we try, he either ignores us or runs away. What're we supposed to do?"

"We could try visiting his house.", suggested Olivia.

The other two stared at her eyebrows raised, surprised that she of all people had suggested that.

"Uh- are you sure?", said Kent. "Won't your mom, y'know, try to kill you again if you don't go home right away?"

"Does that matter? I'm not going to lose one of my friends because I was too scared to do anything about it.", said Olivia. "People like us need to stick together."

"How about we see if he wants to talk today? Or ask Mr. Anderson. He's the only one who would want to help.", said Kent.

Unfortunately for them, John had already lost the will to talk. His friends wanted to talk with him, but he was stuck in his own reality. In his thoughts they hated him and wanted nothing to do with him. Whenever they tried to speak to him during classes, he would lay down and shut them out. When they tried to corner him in the hallways, he would sprint to the other side of the school. In the end, John had managed to evade them long enough for them to give up trying to talk with him... but that didn't mean they were going to give up entirely.

"Can you help us then?", asked Olivia.

"Well, John's just acting like he used to right? Back to a - how should I say this... a socially challenged nerd.", said Mr. Anderson.

"Wow, that's a pretty messed up thing to say...", said Kent.

"I'm just looking at him objectively.", said Mr. Anderson simply. "He was a socially challenged nerd, then around the time after winter recess he became a much more outgoing and friendly guy. And then something must have happened to turn him into such a violent sociopath."

"Well, I dunno why he started hanging out with us, but when he beat up Randall in the bathroom, he was really angry.", replied Marcus.

"Angry?"

"Shaking with rage and trying to kill Randall. Really freaking angry.", described Kent. "I don't think many people know what actually happened. It's not like he's going to go around saying, 'the kid I used to bully just kicked my butt' to everyone is he?"

"And then the entire week he began beating up people that hung around Dylan and his friends.", added Marcus. "Now everyone seems to leave him alone. Dylan doesn't even bully him anymore."

"And then?"

"And nothing. A few days ago he just… stopped. John went back to the way he used to be. Not talking to anyone, just wandering about aimlessly.", said Olivia. "Whenever we try to talk to him, he just runs away or completely ignores us. What should we do?"

Mr. Anderson thought deeply. John was always a student that he tried to look out for without making the other students think he was receiving preferential treatment. Unlike the other kids, he actively tried to be alone. He refused help for any of his problems. A life that was just depressing to even think about. Yet, John changed. What could have possibly caused him to change?

"I don't know… but that doesn't mean you have to give up on trying.", said Mr. Anderson.

And try they did, but John started caring much less with every passing day. It had gotten to the point where he didn't show a single sign of noticing them. Even when visiting his house or calling him, he never answered. As his parents were never home when they visited, they couldn't even talk with him through them.

"We're not getting anywhere…", sighed Olivia, head planted on the table. "It'd be so much easier if we could talk to his parents…"

"Come on Luke, can't you just let me copy your homework? I haven't been able to do mine in a while.", asked Marcus.

Unlike everyone else, Luke was the only one that didn't look exhausted.

"No, why would I let you do that? Just do it right now."

"But I'm tiiired…", he groaned.

"Are you guys still trying to get John to talk again? Give it a rest. He's too far gone.", said Luke.

"What? How could you say that Luke?", said Olivia more surprised than angry that Luke had just said that.

"Yeah, what's wrong with you. He's your friend, wouldn't you want your friends to care if something bad happened to you?", added Marcus.

"What's wrong with *me*? What's wrong is YOU? Look at yourself Olivia. You're trying to hide your bruises with that hoodie, and your lips have been busted.", said Luke. "And you guys. Kent's been kicked off the basketball team for missing too many meetings. Marcus's grades have fell off a cliff."

"And what about it?"

"And what of hurting yourselves to help someone who doesn't notice your efforts?"

"It doesn't matter whether he notices or not!", spat Kent. "We're — "

"If he doesn't care, then what you're doing is a pointless waste of your time and energy.", he stated bluntly.

"I can't believe you would say that Luke. Wouldn't you want your friends to be there for you if you were in his shoes?", said Olivia indignantly.

"Yes, I would. But I wouldn't want them to put themselves in harm's way. What are you going to do when your mom snaps and does something that hiding will be the least of your worries?"

"And you, Kent. You got kicked off the basketball team, and for what? It's not like your grades are picking up either, in fact they're dropping."

"And let's not forget Marcus. What are you going to do when you get held back a year because your grades have plummeted to the point where you're at risk of failing half of your classes?"

"It's not even as if this is just some kind of act so you can feel better about yourselves. You guys are actually throwing your lives away for absolutely no reason. At this rate even if you had made any progress with John, you'll all have either guaranteed being held back a year or worse.", continued Luke. "You people are insane."

They all stared as Luke walked out of the library, stunned by what Luke had just said.

Olivia stared at him with her mouth open. She didn't know whether to feel shocked or angry at what had just happened and couldn't even form a response, but she knew why Luke had said what he did. The bruises on her arm had been getting worse and wearing a sweater on a hot day was bound to bring attention towards her.

But nothing would deter them. Deep down each of them felt a nagging sensation telling them they would regret it forever if they didn't try, and that was enough for them to keep at it. They knew the pain of being stuck in their own mental prisons. They knew the despair and hopelessness that came along with it. Nobody deserved to suffer through that, especially not someone who had already suffered from it before, someone who was their friend.

John wandered the halls quietly, the soles of his shoes sliding on the ground with every step to make as little sound as possible. He looked around for signs of any other student but saw nobody.

'What the heck am I doing?', John thought to himself. His body began instinctively walking towards the entrance of the school, as if it knew he was afraid of being seen by the others. Unfortunately for him he was seen, just not by the people he once considered friends.

"Hey Dylan, John left the school. Should we follow him?", said one of his lackeys. Dylan smirked. He liked pummeling John. Unlike his other victims John didn't cry loudly or scream every time he hit them. Instead he would look at him teary-eyed while shaking in rage. Watching that was much more entertaining than the actual beating or the crying of his other victims.

"I was planning on roughing up Luke today, but I guess I won't.", he responded, hiding his excitement from his goons. It had been a while since he had jumped John and he knew John had beaten up some of his lackeys. They, on the other hand, didn't bother hiding their excitement. Their thirst for vengeance was about to be sated and reclaim their place as the group the other students were afraid of.

Chapter 11: Comeuppance

John walked home as normal.

'Another meaningless day…', he thought. Once again his life was unfulfilling. Strangely enough, the thought didn't depress him. As far as John could remember, his life was shrouded in a thick fog. No goals, no people, nothing in sight. Only recently did he manage to find his way out of it through effort and determination alone. But now he could feel himself slipping back into that same fog. In his mind, the only way to keep himself out of it would be to embrace the loneliness. That was the conclusion he had arrived at, the only way to not despair.

He decided to walk to the park nearby the school. Almost completely empty during this time, and his favorite bench was empty. John had been spending time here whenever he could just to feel more at ease with himself.

Today however, he didn't even get a moment to relax before someone snuck up on him from behind and put him in a headlock as soon as he got comfortable.

"Long time no see John. Miss me?", sneered Dylan. John barely managed to catch a glimpse of him before Dylan's fist smashed right into his chest. As soon as the first hit had landed, multiple hands and feet began striking John repeatedly everywhere.

"Aaargh!", He screamed. The pain and surprise made him jump forward into the dirt, but it didn't stop their hands and feet from meeting him. Just as suddenly as the barrage started, it ended as he was hoisted up by his arms.

"WHAT ARE YOU DOING!?", John roared at them right before he got punched in the stomach. With each punch the crowd cheered louder and the ones grabbing his arms twisted them harder.

Why, of all times, did Dylan and his group decide to jump him? It had been weeks since John had gotten his vengeance, and Dylan hadn't bothered him for months! Would they really hold a grudge for that long? John tried to pull his arms free, but their grasps were too strong, and Dylan wasn't letting up. His only choice was bracing himself.

"OH!", they yelled, as Dylan punched John right in the nose. Blood was trickling down John's bruised face, but he didn't stop there. Another punch thrown here and there, then one right into his stomach. Dylan then grabbed him by his shirt and threw him onto the dirt once more. John laid on ground, coughing from the pain. As he tried to get up to fight back, someone kicked him in the back causing the rest of Dylan's lackeys to join in on the assault.

The beating had gone on for what felt like an eternity. Those vicious thugs were getting their revenge for John's revenge and held nothing back. John tried to curl up to the best of his ability, but it didn't lessen the pain at all. To add insult to injury, they grabbed his bag and emptied its contents right on top of him as they pummeled him. Once they were finally satisfied with the damage they had caused, they left John's battered and bruised body in the dirt.

Only one person remained beside John as the others left. John tried to get up only to get kicked once more.

"You think I forgot?", said Randall, kicking John again. Randall didn't let up. He continued beating John repeatedly, kicking him over and over in the head and chest. John was already in a lot of pain from the earlier beating, so Randall's weak attacks had hurt more than they should have.

"Stop already.", John groaned.

"Oh you want me to stop don't you!? I won't!", he shouted. Randall knelt down and grasped John's throat and began punching his head. John didn't understand why Randall was so angry. He had already received his comeuppance, but Randall still wasn't finished.

"Beg me to stop, you piece of trash! You do anything again and I'm going to kill you!", he screeched at him, pounding at John's head.

"Who are you going to kill?", Marcus bellowed.

"Hit him again and I'm going to break your freaking legs.", growled Kent, who had just shoved Randall off of John. "Get out of here."

"Damn, John! What did they do to you?", asked Kent, helping him up from the ground.

"They really messed him up bad…", said Marcus, picking up John's belongings and shoving them back into his bag.

"Why… why are you guys here?", muttered John.

The duo looked at each other for a moment before laughing.

"Dude, what do you even mean? Of course we'd be here.", said Kent, letting John down onto the bench.

"Yeah, what good are friends if they aren't around when you're down?", added Marcus. "We heard those punks leaving the park laughing about you, so we came to check on you."

"I thought you guys didn't want to hang around me anymore.", asked John.

"What?"

"Remember when I beat up Randall way back when and you guys were on my case about me beating up the others."

"Wait, that's why you stopped hanging out with us? Because of that?", asked Kent.

"Well yeah? Why wouldn't we be? You do something stupid and your friends 'll call you out for it.", said Marcus.

John looked down, saying absolutely nothing. Could he really believe that? That he was holding himself back? It sounded too good to be true.

"pfft- hehehe AHAHAHAHAHAHAHAHAHAHAHA!", laughed John who was now both laughing and crying at the same time.

"Whoa, what's wrong!?", asked Kent.

"Nothing's wrong. Everything's all right!", said John, wiping the blood and tears off his face. "Never felt better."

"Aaaaah!", he yelled out, stretching his arms. John had felt like he had just woken up from a terrible nightmare, or rather as if his soul had been poured right back into his husk of a body. The cuts and bruises on his body still stung but the pain wasn't anywhere near as bad as it was a few minutes earlier. He got up and began limping towards the entrance of the park. Despite being beaten an inch away from unconsciousness, John had never felt more alive.

"Need help getting home or are you okay?", asked Kent who held his hand out to John.

"I'm fine. Thanks.", he responded.

John limped down the road towards his house. Anyone seeing him would have thought he was going mad with how much he was laughing. John immediately began remembering everything he had thought weeks ago in an attempt to avoid his friends. Once he realized how meaningless those thoughts were, he just couldn't help but laugh at his foolishness.

The moment John entered his home, fatigue washed over him. After dropping his bag in the living room, he limped his way towards the bathroom. He took one look at the mirror and began laughing once more. His bruised, bloodstained face had an ear-to-ear grin that just made his face look even sillier. John was too overjoyed to feel any hatred for the people who had hurt him. He still hated them, but that hatred had the intensity of a small candle in the tempest of joy. Even the pain when dressing his wounds didn't change that.

'Why do you assume they want you to apologize? They are your friends. They invited you to their circle for a reason...'

"Man I should have just listened.", John thought aloud.

"But you didn't."

John turned his head to see Smith staring down at him with the smuggest expression he had seen yet.

"Came to rub that in?"

"No. I just wanted to see how pathetic you'd end up looking.", answered Smith. "But it seems to have turned out for the better in your case. You would have learned nothing if you didn't suffer first. It's funny really."

"What is?"

"You."

"Huh?", responded John.

"Everything you do leads you to worse suffering. But that isn't what's funny. Despite all the suffering you've put yourself through, you haven't ever given up hope. That is funny."

"But I did give up. I gave up on my friends, but they didn't give up on me.", responded John. What on earth did Smith mean?

"Are you sure? If you had truly given up on them, why did you stick around to talk with them instead of running, er limping, away?

Deep down you never gave up hoping that you would return back to your little circle of friends.”

“And it’s not just that moment either. How long has it been since you started exercising routinely? You wanted to end it all before then, but you never gave up hope on getting vengeance.”

“I wouldn’t call that hope. More like rage.”, said John quietly.

“You wanted for revenge and you needed to get it yourself. Or should I say you wished for it? It was more than just simple mindless rage or hatred. If that wasn’t hope what would you call it?”, asked Smith.

“I dunno? You’d normally never see anyone use the word hope with words like hatred or rage. It just doesn’t, I don’t know, sound right?”

“Look at yourself. You took all that hatred you had for your bullies and pointed it towards a dream. Brick by brick, you laid the foundations to achieve that dream. The you now is different from the you a year ago. Be proud of your achievement.”, said Smith, walking towards the open window.

“This room was once the prison outside of your mental prison. You turned it into a workshop where you reforged yourself into a completely different person.”

"What are you trying to say?", asked John. It felt oddly embarrassing hearing someone compliment him. He had rarely received compliments much less ones that were genuine, but that wasn't the point. What was Smith getting at with all this?

"For someone who is so hopeful, you have a pretty pessimistic outlook."

"Like I said, it isn't hope. It's my hatred.", responded John intensely.

"I couldn't care less about what you want to call it. Your defeatist, pessimistic attitude every time you falter is holding you back. Break those chains and stand tall. Look at yourself, ADMIRE yourself. Remember how far you walked to get here!"

"You got here all on your own. Nobody carried you to this point. My coercion would have been meaningless if you decided to ignore me."

John stood up from his bed and walked towards his dresser. A very fine layer of dust coated the surface since it had been a while since anyone had wiped it down. There was a picture frame with an image of his family from a year ago in it. A couple trying to force a smile while a sad, weak-looking boy frowned and tried to look as small as possible.

He looked up towards the mirror on the dresser and it was a completely different person.

John rarely paid any attention to the changes in his physique, even if he knew they were happening. The picture put into perspective how great the magnitude of change was. The pale, flimsy looking body of the boy in the photo had completely changed. Even the depressed face had transformed to something more *normal*, despite the bruises and drop of blood coming out of one of his nostrils. He flexed his muscles, both instinctively and out of curiosity.

"Do you get it now? You can do anything you put your mind to. All that's left for you is to shake off your pessimistic attitude and keep walking forward. Be unstoppable!"

"You really think I have that in me?", said John, smiling at his reflection.

"Who knows? Someone must have the ability, the drive, the will…", said Smith, floating out of the window. "And it's up to you to make sure that someone is YOU."

Chapter 12: Luke

The next day came by in a blink of an eye. It had taken him a while yesterday to calm his parents down after they saw his face, but it made sleeping much easier.

"Aaaaah…", he groaned as he stretched himself. The things Smith had told him the other day had stuck in his mind. There was no school today, so John decided to go for a jog. The air was cool, but not too cool. The sun was bright, but not too strong. It was the perfect day for jogging. The park where he jogged around was mostly empty this early in the morning. This meant there would be nobody to disturb him other than his own thoughts… or so he thought. John jogged for ninety minutes before he was finally tired.

"Huff… huff… that should be good enough.", said John, sweating profusely. It was still early, so he decided to sit in the bench he usually sat on… but it was already occupied. Another boy of comparable age was sitting in it with his head in his hands.

"Huh, Luke is that you?", asked John.

Luke's head shot up from his hands and he immediately ran away.

'The heck was that about? Why'd he run after seeing me?', he thought. The creeping feeling from before was coming back along with the thoughts.

'No. I'm not going to go back there… I won't let that happen. I'll try to talk with him on Monday.'

John headed home, still thinking about what had just happened. Maybe he assumed too much when Kent and Marcus consoled him the day before. Or maybe he did something he couldn't remember a few weeks ago that must have offended Luke in some way. Either way something was wrong, and he wanted to know why. He wasn't going to wait around for life to happen around him this time. Luke was very different from the brash duo, and from his reaction he wasn't too keen on wanting to start a conversation with John. It was time for John to take matters into his own hands and start that conversation.

John returned home to complete his workout but what happened at the park stuck with him, distracting him. Even though he decided to talk to him, he didn't know what to talk about. He didn't know anything other than maybe schoolwork that he had in common with any of his friends. Most of his hobbies were what normal people thought as strange or, if they were being honest, downright creepy.

"John! Where were you, we were so worried!", his mother shrieked.

"Relax! I just went for a jog!", he answered.

"Tell us before you go outside! What if something happened to you!? How would we know!?"

"I'm fiiiine! The park is like ten minutes away!", he said, running up the stairs into his room before his mother could continue arguing with him. He was too busy thinking about Luke to care about how worried his mother was.

"If only I could have just ran after him", he thought aloud.

"But you could have done that.", said Smith, appearing behind him.

"I could have, but I'd feel like a jerk if I put him on the spot like that. And it might end up making him angrier or whatever's going on with him.", responded John, who at this point was no longer fazed by Smith appearing out of nowhere.

"You'd rather go through the same ordeal as before?", asked Smith. "You know Luke won't come to you; you'll have to go to him."

"I *know* that, but how can I talk to him without angering him? We have barely anything in common with each other."

"Talk about schoolwork then. It's something you both have in common, and he's always trying to complete his in the library. That's the perfect time for you to confront him.", he suggested.

"That sounds awfully generic don't you think?", said John, furrowing his brow.

"Does it matter? It's your best shot at talking to him.", responded Smith.

"Tch, fine. I'll do that then."

The event stayed on his mind during the entire weekend. Unlike before, it didn't depress him or anything. It actually made him think deeply about what could possibly be on Luke's mind. John knew very little about people he considered "normal". Unlike most of his other friends, Luke was also much more distant. For John, trying to understand what might be going through a mind of another person wasn't just hard. It was impossible.

'No point thinking about it. The only thing I can do is just ask him tomorrow.', he thought, turning over in his bed.

John walked to school as usual the next day and as usual he arrived early. Much to his surprise multiple students kept glancing at him. John recognized some of Dylan's lackeys scowling at him from a distance, which was also strange seeing how they usually sneered every time they saw him after giving him a beating not to mention rarely being on time. John paid it no mind, he had more important things to do than glower back, but it didn't hurt to mock them with a smirk.

As usual, John was the first to arrive to the classroom followed closely by Olivia.

"John! Are you okay!?", she gasped.

"Yeah?", he responded, surprised.

"Sorry, let me catch my breath – Kent told me you got jumped last week, and I heard some other people talking about it too!"

"Why the heck would anyone care to talk about stuff like that? Dylan must jump a new person every other day.", asked John.

"So did you. Why else would they have talked about it?"

'But I stopped that like a month ago! Do people really remember things like that?', thought John.

"They said they beat you until you were bleeding, but you look like nothing changed.", said Olivia, examining John's face.

"Well what can I say? I heal quickly. Speaking of quickly, where's Luke? He's usually here by now."

"That's odd. I thought I saw him at the entrance of the school."

Their conversation slowly died as the other students began flooding the classroom. As John expected, the other students began whispering about him, some even outright asking him whether or not he was actually attacked, but John paid it no mind. He was starting to get a bit worried as Luke still hadn't shown up yet. Even stranger yet, when he did show up, he immediately started scowling at John.

'Oh, he's angry.', he thought. *'But why? We haven't spoken with each other in almost a month!'*

The day continued on until recess. Now was the time to act and see what was the problem with Luke. Fortunately for John, it was easy enough to locate him.

"Here goes…", John muttered to himself before approaching Luke.

"Hey Luke! How's things?", he said.

"What d'you want?", Luke responded, now glaring at the papers in front of him.

"What? I just wanted talk about the homework. I just needed help –"

"No you don't.", he interjected.

"Aww come on, don't be like that. How about you let me see yours?"

"I'm not going to let you copy my homework. Go away, you're bothering me and I'm busy."

"Dude, can't we just talk?", said John. He was getting slightly ticked off now but kept his patience. He would get nowhere if he just snapped at Luke.

"Look, I told you I'm *busy*. Can't you find someone else to bother?", he grumbled.

"Alright, relax. I'll just sit here.", John quickly replied.

John's suspicions were proven correct. Luke was angry with him for some reason. Or maybe he really was busy, and John was just bothering him. A few minutes later Olivia entered the library, immediately spotting John and Luke.

"Hey guys! Oh Luke you're doing the homework? Mind if I take a quick look?", said Olivia.

"Sure.", replied Luke, smiling at her.

"You let her see your work but not me? That's messed up."

Luke's eyebrows furrowed in annoyance, but just as quickly as they had, he stopped. Suddenly he grabbed a few sheets of paper and passed them to John.

"Fine, look at it. Just don't copy word for word."

"Thanks.", he replied. John had already completed his work, but since Olivia was here he didn't want to talk about what had happened yesterday. Instead he needed to find something else to talk about, and what better than the assignment that Luke had just handed to him?

'Why does Luke have so many of the same assignment?', he suddenly thought. He looked at the name on the paper, and sure enough, it wasn't Luke's name nor was it one he recognized.

"You sell homework?", asked John.

"If you're done looking at it then give it back.", snapped Luke, snatching the paper from his hands.

"Here you go. Thanks Luke!", said Olivia, also handing back the paper she took.

"No problem!", Luke said, smiling at her.

John wasn't thick enough to not see that Luke was smitten with Olivia, quite a few students were. It just wasn't important at the moment. Why was Luke selling homework? He dressed much better than the average student, not to mention groomed better. Compared to the others, Luke's family was pretty well-off. He didn't need to engage in such conspicuous rule breaking, regardless of if most teachers couldn't care less about it, just to make a little money.

Luke noticed John scrutinizing him and grabbed all of his belongings before exiting the library. John, being as nimble and quiet as he could possibly be, followed after him. Luke was in trouble, and he was his friend. The least he could do was make sure he was okay. What else were friends for? As classes ended and everyone began going home, John waited. Strangely, Luke was also waiting. Luke waited so long that most of the students excluding the ones part of teams and clubs had already left.

"Ey Luke!", a boy yelled. John recognized the voice and his hatred flared to life. He would recognize Dylan's friends anywhere.

"Oh hi Mark.", Luke responded timidly. "Here's your answers for the algebra, science, and history classes."

"Good looks.", the thuggish boy responded. "Do my girl's homework next aight?"

"I don't know if I got the time, I still haven't done mine…", Luke started saying until he saw the taller boy stare him down. "Alright, I'll do it. Just give it to me."

"Do mine's too.", said the taller boy, thrusting some papers onto Luke.

John couldn't watch any more. He didn't know what they had on Luke, but he sure wasn't going to sit back and let them push him around.

"What do you punks think you're doing?", shouted John, walking quickly towards them.

"What d'you want?", the taller boy jeered.

"I want you to do your own freaking homework.", he hissed.

"What are you talking about?", the other boy sneered. "Luke said he was going to do it for us. Ain't that right?"

"Yeah… I did.", responded Luke, glaring and John.

"And I'm saying he doesn't want to!", snarled John, throwing the papers back into the taller boy's face.

Before the boy could react, John shoved him onto the ground. He cared little about going for the "out of bounds" areas, especially for friends of Dylan, and immediately kicked the taller boy right between the legs as hard as he possibly could. Once his friend attempted to retaliate, John punched the thuggish boy in the eye and began pummeling him relentlessly. There was no time for mercy, not when these hooligans were threatening his friend.

"You make Luke do any of your work again and next time I'm going to freaking break you, you hear me?", he roared at them.

"You think you're tough now John? Watch your back for the beating Dylan's going to give you.", the thuggish boy groaned.

"Yeah, go cry to Dylan you freaking coward.", he mocked.

As Dylan's lackeys ran away, John turned to face Luke expecting him to be happy. He definitely did not expect Luke to be gritting his teeth in anger.

"What do you think you're doing!?", Luke growled.

"What? I saw them messing with you, so I stopped them."

"Oh wow! Thanks for helping me!", he responded sarcastically.

"What's going on, why're you acting so weird lately? First you stop talking with me and now you're complaining I defended you from those jerks?", asked John.

"Damn it John, screw off already!", Luke shouted. "You think you're so cool now don't you?!"

"What did you say?", exclaimed John. Then it finally hit him. All those assignments Luke was always completing, everything. "No freaking way, don't tell me you were kissing up to them!? Oh my GOD!"

"Yeah, I was. What's the big deal?", retorted Luke. "Now that you're no longer the most unpopular kid in school, I AM! I am NOT going to let myself get jumped every other day like you did."

"I couldn't care less about popularity. This entire time I thought you were selling your homework. I didn't think you were *this* pathetic."

"We're going to see who's pathetic when you're crawling on the ground after Dylan jumps you again!"

"You're such a freaking idiot. They'll never accept you as one of them. Didn't you see how those two morons treat you?", John said coldly. A bitter taste began permeating his mouth making his face look even more disgusted.

John walked away rigidly before he had lost his temper on him. Strangely enough, John didn't feel betrayed by what Luke had just said. If anything, he expected it somewhat. He had always wondered why Luke was strangely so distant compared to his other friends, and he finally knew why. This was the first time John had ever lost someone he called a friend.

Chapter 13: Luke, Again

As John paced around his room, he began remembering every moment he spoke with Luke. The time when Luke was surprised John had gotten into a fight? He was actually thinking that John would overtake him in popularity! All that classwork he was doing? Just to brownnose some punks that couldn't care less about him. Yet despite all that, John couldn't bring himself to dislike him, even if Luke was helping the same people that bullied him. Luke was just looking out for himself. In a way, he wasn't that different from John before.

"How did it go?", asked Smith.

"Terribly. I can't believe Luke was sucking up to those guys.", John replied, laying on his bed.

"All this time I thought we were friends, but really it was only me. I just can't believe he actually hated me for being more 'popular' than he was.", John began to vent. "Over freaking 'popularity', *really*!? Does he really think people will like him if he kisses up to the same group that terrorizes the entire school!?"

John shot up from his bed and began pacing around his room in anger. He might not have hated Luke, but he was definitely angry with what he had learned.

"Everyone cares about popularity, even you. It's pretty hypocritical of you to judge him so harshly because of it.", said Smith.

"Huh? Why would I care about being popular?"

"You care. You might not care as much as someone like Luke, but you definitely care about popularity. You were very interested when you heard people were talking about you weren't you?", explained Smith. "You've seen the benefits that come with popularity. The respect, the ability to safely walk through the school without being harassed by other students… anyone could see why Luke would want that."

"I *know* that. I just don't see why anyone would throw away their dignity just to be more popular. I don't see the others doing the same thing.", responded John. "Heck, Kent used to be on the basketball team, yet he's in the library with the rest of the school's social outcasts."

"You know the answer to that. The school's hierarchy is out of whack. The most popular students look out for each other and, excluding outliers like when you went on a rampage, the only way to climb that social hierarchy is by befriending them.", explained Smith. "Luke knows that, but he hasn't had to deal with them as much as you have. He doesn't know that they're scum that'll use him forever."

"Why don't you talk to him tomorrow? That is, if you care enough to.", suggested Smith.

John considered the thought. Except there was one glaring problem. Luke was so obsessed with popularity he might not even want to listen. Especially not to John. He did after all want him to get beaten down again by Dylan. But if there was anyone that could convince Luke, it was John himself. As arrogant as he thought it sounded, there was no other choice. Even he wasn't so socially incompetent to not know of the backlash getting someone else to talk to him might cause, and in his warped idea of friendship only fueled his desire to repair their relationship.

John still had an entire day to mull over his decision. Was it the right one? He didn't know. Was it one he would be happy with? Hopefully. Would he be able to change Luke's mind? Probably not, but if there was even a single opportunity to make his friend come to his senses, he would take it. Luke was one of the first people to ever have a conversation with him, one of the first people to ever acknowledge his existence. He wasn't just going to let him slip away that easily.

Morning arrived much sooner than John thought. The overcast sky and chilling breeze seemed to match his emotions to a tee.

"Hey! John, wait up!", someone yelled behind him. It was Luke!

"Thanks – wait, lemme catch my breath.", he wheezed. "Sorry about that. And sorry for yesterday". John's heart filled with joy after he heard him say that. Maybe this'll be easier than he thought.

"It's just, I feel bad about all that stuff I said yesterday. I don't know what made me say that."

"It's alright. I don't mind. I'm sorry 'bout what I said too.", John replied. "We can just forget it happened right?"

"Sure. Want to cut through the park? It'll be faster.", Luke suggested.

"Why not?", responded John. As they walked, John suddenly remembered something. "Remember a few days ago when I saw you and you ran from me? What was that about?"

"Oh nothing, I always do that when I see someone outside of the school. Just feels awkward y'know?", said Luke, slowing down to a crawl. Something was wrong, but John was too busy being happy with reconciling with Luke that he wasn't paying attention.

"What's the hold up? Let's – oof!", said John as he was shoved onto the ground. John wasn't able to get up before someone kicked him in the face.

"What the – ouch!", yelled John as he was being hit repeatedly by two people. John looked up to see Luke walking away. He knew what had just happened, but he couldn't believe that Luke had helped whoever his assailants were, most likely the thugs from yesterday, jump him.

"Hahaha! What an idiot I can't believe he fell for that!", one of the people behind him said, who John recognized as the shorter of the two boys from the other day.

"LUKE! LUKE COME BACK HERE!", John shouted after him.

"Shut up John. Luke ain't bring you here to save you.", a boy, who John recognized as the taller one, barked before kicking him in the side of his ribs. "You're dumber than I thought. You actually believed that crap he told you?"

One of the boys kicked John in the lip, causing it to bleed. John immediately tried to brace himself by covering his head with his arms and curling up to protect his chest from their assault, but they didn't let up. Yet despite the pain of the beating, John's chest hurt much more. He *trusted* Luke! What Luke did hurt more than any beating he could have received. The disappointment he had with Luke was completely gone, replaced with a hatred that burned just as fierce as his hatred for Dylan.

John laid there in the dirt after the two who were beating him were satisfied and left. Even after the pain had mostly subsided, his hatred didn't. Luke's betrayal was the cruelest thing anyone had ever done to him. Dylan may have been a brute that beat his victims senseless, but he stopped there. The psychological damage that Luke had inflicted was a nuclear bomb compared to that.

By the time John had arrived at the school, he was already half an hour late. He had already missed half of his first class.

'Where is that rat? I'm going to rip him apart piece by piece', he thought. The look of rage on his face was enough for everyone to look away from his gaze. Even the students that were laughing quietly about his misfortune went silent immediately after being glared at by him.

"John.", Olivia whispered to him. "What happened to you?"

"Nothing.", he growled. *'That won't be paid back tenfold.'*

"You sound like you're going to kill someone. Come on, you can tell me can't you?"

"Trust me, you *don't* want to know. It'll be much better for you, and for Luke.", he said through gritted teeth.

"Luke?"

"Never mind. Forget you heard that."

The day seemed to get longer with every passing moment. At one point John was so angry that he unconsciously snapped his pencil from squeezing it too hard. The only cure for his anger was ripping Luke apart piece by piece and from the way Luke reacted to his stare, he knew. Luke expected John to behave like every other unpopular kid, lick their wounds and go about their business. John, however, was socially immature with enough physical strength to shred him like paper. His friends gave him a place to belong and caused him to value them highly. Luke, who had just betrayed him in such a cruel and meaningless fashion, had just signed his death warrant.

Once the school day ended, John quickly ran out and began waiting outside the main entrance of the school. There would be no escape for Luke.

'Where is he? He should have left ages ago!', John thought angrily. *'Does he think he can hide from me all day? Does he think I'll forget!?'*

Soon, his 'patience' had paid off as Luke walked out of the school. Strangely enough John wasn't the only one following him. The two pieces of trash that attacked him earlier were with him. Odd. Even if Luke helped them ambush John, there was no reason for them to hang around him. Scum like them expected others to do their bidding. John highly doubted they would let Luke of all people to enter their little clique, so he decided to follow them.

Luke had an expression of utmost terror. Even if he was afraid of what John might do, there was no reason to be so terrified. Fighting or not, John would be hard pressed to fight two people at once despite being stronger than both of them.

"Ey Luke, you got the homework?", the taller boy asked.

"Wh-what? Uh I didn't have the time to do it…", Luke whimpered.

"What?", said the boy, staring Luke down. "Why the hell not? You said you'd have my stuff done during recess."

"Y-yeah but John's been watching me.", he tried to say.

"You scared of him? Your eyes ain't working or something? We're in front of you, and he ain't here.", the other boy growled.

"Okay, I'll do it! I'll have it tomorrow morning.", blurted Luke.

"You better have it or else we're going to have to kick *your -* aaargh!", the boy yelled as he hit the ground. John had ran full speed and kicked him in the back.

While the boy was still reeling from the pain, John kicked him down once more before stomping on his head repeatedly. The taller boy was so shocked that he didn't even react until after John had already stomped on his friend's head twice. The taller boy slugged John right in the face, but all it did was add more fuel to his rage. With his full weight he body slammed the taller boy into the ground before strangling and pummeling the boy.

"John you son of a – I'm gonna break your teeth!", the other boy screamed as he got up. The taller boy's face had been beaten to a pulp and was almost unconscious before his friend tackled John off of him. He was ready for the boy due to his scream and managed to grab him before he could be pinned under the boy's weight. After putting the boy in a chokehold and repeatedly pounding his fist on the boy's face, he had finally yielded to him.

"Alright stop, stop! I'm sorry!", the boy, now teary-eyed, yelled while holding his hands up to cover his face.

"If I ever see you again I'm going to beat you into next week.", he snarled.

Luke was stunned by what he had just witnessed. It hadn't even occurred to him to take the opportunity to run until John's gaze turned towards him, but his legs were frozen in fear.

"Hey John, I-I'm sorry. Those guys made me trick you this morning.", Luke's voice trailed off. "Please, I'm sorry. We can forget this right?"

Listening to Luke, his hatred vanished. Instead, John was disappointed. Even now, Luke only cared about his own skin. Was Luke always this much of a pathetic coward? He was willing to throw away any dignity just to escape a beating? John couldn't bear to look at him anymore.

"They made you lure me?", asked John.

"Y-yeah! I didn't want them to hurt me. I'm sorry man."

John took a deep breath. "That was the worst lie I've ever heard. You really are the slimiest piece of crap I've ever met, and I've met Randall."

"Wait, I'm not lying! I'm serious, I didn't want to man. Please, I'm sorry!", Luke panicked, cowering.

"Get the hell out of my sight before I kick your ass…"

Chapter 14: A Small Photograph

The walk home was an uneventful one. After what had just happened, John had completely given up on Luke. The level of pathetic cowardice that he displayed had disgusted John to the point where he no longer wanted to think about him.

John didn't feel like exercising once he got home. He had already completed a workout on the two punks that jumped him earlier that morning and any more would remind him of Luke, so he decided to play games on his computer. If there was something that could make him blind to all of his problems, it would be a game.

"Anyone online?", he typed.

"In a sec. Busy with something else right now.", responded the ranger.

"Mage must still be at work then right?"

"Yeah. We can still run some of the previous dungeons in the meantime though. Solo-ing without a tank is so annoying."

"That's why I play tank. It's much easier to find parties as a tank.", replied John.

"What's new?"

"What do you mean?", asked John.

"Well ever since a few months ago, you've always complained about something that happened to you in real life. Or you ask us about something.", the ranger typed.

"Really? I never noticed that. that's pretty embarrassing with how you said it and all."

"Yeah, but it's not like we really care. People just need to vent their frustrations and all. Whether it's a forum, a game, or even to nobody, it's always nice to just let it out."

"Thanks man. But I'm fine today."

"Damn. I've been writing down everything you've been saying for the past few months to write a book hahaha!", the ranger confessed.

"You shouldn't have told me that. As if hearing how much I rant about my life wasn't embarrassing enough."

The rest of the day seemed to pass by in the blink of an eye as he enjoyed himself. Had it not been for the front door opening, John would never have noticed how much time had passed. His head quickly turned to look at the window to see the sun setting.

"Thanks for the runs, bye guys!", he quickly typed before logging out.

John quickly thrust his hands into his bag to find his homework crumpled and torn beyond legibility from his earlier scuffle.

"Oh well…", he said out loud.

With his homework in tatters, motivation for exercise gone, and exhaustion from gaming, he had nothing to do. The day was practically over anyway. With nothing else to do, he'd just wait for dinner, go to sleep, and see if he could copy the homework from someone else.

John sighed heavily. Was there really any change from now and before? He was still going through a mindless routine with zero deviation. Eat, sleep, go to school, exercise or fight, repeat. Was there any reason to doing anything if it's all so meaningless?

It had only been a few months since all these changes had happened. Beside his bed was a rack carrying multiple dumbbells with varying weights. The once empty bookshelf holding nothing but old, dusty textbooks and photo albums had been dusted clean and filled with books that he enjoyed reading. Even the dusty rug atop a dusty wooden floor and been vacuumed and mopped, respectively and recently. The only thing that didn't change was his dresser. The single picture frame had been there for years.

The single picture, of a small depressed looking boy between two parents forcing a smile. John stared at it, wondering. How big was the difference between his life now and before? What differences would there be if he never changed to begin with? Would Luke ever have stabbed him in the back? Would Luke, or even any of his friends, ever attempt to befriend him? Would he have ever truly felt the mental anguish of being alone? Would he have ever felt… alive?

In his mind's eye, John could see his old room. The dusty floors, dirty carpet. Cardboard boxes full of things he never bothered to place properly. The cobwebbed ceilings, the way sunlight cast a dusty beam through his window. The emotionless life he lived. Compared to before, the sudden change was almost dreamlike. Who could have foreseen that John would turn his entire life on its head? Certainly not him. Back then all he cared about was sleeping and killing time before falling asleep once more.

John headed down the stairs into the living room where his parents were slouched on the couch. Despite the exhaustion being the same, even they looked different. They would return from their jobs, staring into the distance with their souls being crushed ever so slightly more with every passing day. Now they were happier, even beckoning John to come down from the stairs and sit with them.

"How was today?", his father asked. Even that was different. His father never spoke with him unless he was forced to, but ever since he started changing his father cared much more about him. There was nothing forced about this smile other than hiding his exhaustion.

"Everything alright?", his mother added. He remembered how his mother tried to force him out of his "shell", leading to the creation of the depressing picture atop his dresser. After that, she gave up trying entirely. Had it not been for the breakfast and lunch and the bi-monthly cleaning of his room, nobody would think anyone lived in his room.

"Fine. I just came down here to see you.", he replied. A few months ago, this conversation would never have happened and if by some freak chance it had, he would have never responded to anything they would have said. Instead, he would have just bolted up the stairs into his room and closed the door.

"That's good... good.", said his father yawning. "It's good that you're fine..."

"Whew, I guess I'll order something for dinner, I am tired!", his mother said. "What do you want John?"

"Uh, I don't know. I can't remember what's good.", he lied. The truth would have been 'I don't know. I've never eaten fast food in my life.', but he didn't want to ruin the mood.

"Oh well. I guess I'll just buy a pizza, or Chinese."

An awkward silence passed between them for almost ten minutes. Though his parents' attitudes towards him changed, they still knew very little about him. His likes, dislikes? They couldn't remember. They've been spending so much time drowning themselves in their work to forget that he existed when he was a pathetic failure.

"How's school?", his dad blurted out in an attempt to start a conversation.

"Not bad?"

"You get into any fights yet? Planning on getting into any fights?"

"John don't listen to your father. As long as you're safe that's okay." his mother responded, shocked that his father would mention such a thing.

"Well… there was one time."

"ALRIGHT!", his father shouted. "I knew it!"

"John…", his mother sighed. "At least you aren't instigating any fights, right?"

"No… I'm not.", he said.

"AHA!", his mother yelled this time. "I told you John was a good boy!"

"What about any friends? How are your friends like?", asked his father.

"Er…", he started. At that moment he realized he didn't know much about his friends either. How would his parents react to him saying all of his friends are the misfits of the school? Sure his friends had been there for him when he needed them, but he knew nothing much about them other than that.

"They're nice people, always helping me out. Even when I'm down, they've been there even when they have their own problems.", said John.

"Why don't you bring your friends over some day? We'd love to see them.", said his mother.

"Or if you want to go to your friend's house, just tell us.", his father added. "We really need to get him a phone someday.", his father muttered to his mother before the doorbell began ringing.

"Wow, they delivered that faster than I thought!", exclaimed his mother. His father opened the door and set down two boxes with a large bottle of soda that frothed from the movement.

John never ate pizza in his life, so he waited for his parents to mimic how they ate. It tasted delicious! The greasy texture, the taste, the way it melted in his mouth. To think something like this existed! He never tasted anything like it. The reheated breakfast and lunch he ate every day tasted bland. He still thought his mother's dinner tasted better, but the experience of eating something new seemed to blow his mind away.

"That pizza tasted better than I thought it would.", said John, opening the bottle slowly to prevent it from spilling out.

"It's been a while since we've sat here together, just talking.", his father said aloud.

"A few months, really. We've been so busy with work…", his mother started saying. "It's getting late now, John. You have school tomorrow don't you?"

"Okay, fine…", he said.

John returned to his room to find the picture frame flat on his dresser. He stretched his arm out, attempting to put the frame back in position before considering throwing it out. In the end, he decided to leave it the way it was. The past was the past. There was no use being dwelling on it. John had changed, and that small picture would serve as a reminder forever on how much he had changed.

Downstairs, his parents were still awake, thinking.

"Why are we still working such long hours?"

"As much as I don't to say it, we did it because we hated John.", his father said quietly.

"John changed, no thanks to us.", his mother lamented. "He's growing up to be a strong and healthy boy."

"We don't know that for sure. He's changed a lot but, as pathetic as it sounds, we know nothing about him."

"And we never will if we spend most of our day throwing ourselves into our work without spending any time on this family!"

"Do you think he'll let us? How many years have we just neglected him and left him to rot?", asked his father. "It's been years since we've went anywhere with him. All those wasted vacations that we never took because we hated him."

"Don't say it like that", she pleaded.

"What other way is there to say it? We were never there for him. Everything he's done he did it all alone. We've never went to any of the parent teacher conferences. I don't think I've ever stepped foot in his school!"

He looked at her somberly. "Do you remember when we went on that fishing outing? We sat there for an hour waiting for John to say something. And he didn't! I randomly said I knew there was something on his mind. What if he said nothing?"

His mother sighed. "When you called John down to sit with us, he didn't run back to his room. He sat with us. He was willing to talk about himself. Did you see how he ate that pizza? That was the first time he's probably ever eaten anything that wasn't a home cooked meal. And he said *nothing*. John's trying his hardest, and it's time we did too. We can never undo what we've done, but we can at least try…"

"You're right. We owe it to him."

Chapter 15: Panic

John had listened in on his parents' entire conversation that night. He didn't know how to react to what he had just heard. Angry because of what they had admit? Surprised and saddened that he never realized it? Or should he feel happy knowing they were going to change?

'This is just a sick, sick dream! That's it right? I fell asleep once I got back here!', he thought. John laid on his bed trying to fall asleep, but to no avail. He just couldn't stop thinking about what he had just heard. The air around him seemed to get hotter and heavier. His body started sweating profusely and shaking!

John raised his hands, visibly shaking, and clenched them into fists. *'NO! I told myself I wasn't going to let myself go back there!'*. He began slapping his face, to distract himself. But nothing was going to make him forget what he heard. John cried silently to sleep.

The next morning came too early. His parents were still home, and he could hear them moving about. In fact, they were coming up to his door.

"John are you awake yet?", asked his mother through the door.

"Mmrrph"

"What? I'm opening the door.", she responded. "Had trouble sleeping? Your eyes are bloodshot."

"Yes.", he croaked.

"Alright, I won't pester you then. Come down when you want to have breakfast."

"Leave in microwave…"

Right now he wouldn't be able to see his parents without lashing out with rage or crying again. It'd be easier to just wait until they had left for work. By the time they had left, the breakfast had become lukewarm.

John walked to school but took a longer path and walked much slower than usual. He wanted to let his mind rest. Could he really be angry at his parents for what they've admitted to doing? Until they said it, he hadn't even noticed how they treated him. As far back as he could remember, he saw it as a blessing as it meant he could play games longer. He had given up on everything long before his parents had given up on him.

He spat on the ground in disgust. What was he thinking? He's been blaming himself for everything recently, or even trying to understand the motives of others. That kind of thinking was what allowed Luke to lure him into the park to get jumped. How could he just throw all of the blame on himself? They were his parents! How could they admit they gave up on him completely so easily and still have the audacity to face him like nothing happened? There's no way he'd let himself become a door mat for everyone to walk over. If he did, there would have been no point in him to strengthen himself to such a degree.

John had barely made it in time to not be late for his first class. Strangely enough, Olivia didn't make it either. She was usually the first to make it to school and even on days when she was late, she always made it in time before the first class began. He began leaning towards Luke who was next to him, but then tried to play it off as if he was just stretching. He'd have to wait until later to find out anything.

Olivia showed up for their second period class in the most bizarre outfit possible. Despite the sweltering heat of a classroom in the middle of a hot spring day, she was dressed as if she expected it to snow. There were beads of sweat rolling down her face being absorbed by the thick scarf wrapped around her neck and mouth. The other students attempted to laugh as quietly as possible, but not John. He knew why she wore all those clothes.

John leaned over towards her. "Are you okay?"

Olivia didn't respond. Instead she began scribbling away at a small index card. As she extended her arm over to his desk, she quickly pulled it back and scribbled on the index card once more.

'~~No, I'm not okay. I need to talk to someone. I don't know how much of my mother I can tolerate.~~

I'm fine.'

John could barely decipher what she had crossed out multiple times, but he didn't need to. Something was clearly wrong, and she desperately needed help. John turned the card over, wrote something on it, and passed it back.

'When do you want to talk?'

She quickly wrote her answer and held it up to him.

'Wait for me after school.'

And so he did. The classes droned on and Olivia's scarf had become drenched with her sweat. By the time recess came around, Olivia looked like she could keel over at any moment. Olivia threw herself at the library door to open it, dragged her heels across the floor, and flopped gracelessly into a chair. Luke shifted uncomfortably in his seat while watching her struggle but did nothing else. John tried to walk to her, but she laboriously held up the index card.

"Wait… after… school.", she breathed.

John's patience was wearing thin. Were classes always this long? The longer he stared at the clock, the slower it felt. Sometimes he could have sworn he saw the hands of the clock move back. The moment the school day was over, he immediately rushed out, stopping by a vending machine before he did so. He waited by the entrance as multiple students flooded out. It seemed like every student had left and John was beginning to think he had just missed her until Olivia shambled out of the school, dragging her feet inches with every step.

"Here you go.", said John, holding out a cold drink.

She took the bottle and drank it all in less than a minute. "Thank you."

"So what did you want to talk about?"

"I – never mind.", she began before walking away.

"Wait!", John grabbed her arm only for her to wince in pain. "Oh sorry! But just say *something* at least."

Olivia stared at him somberly before she removed her scarf revealing an ugly bruise across her jaw. She then began to roll up her sleeves. Both arms had been cut and burned repeatedly. Then she removed her gloves, showing how her fingers had been mangled. It was a horrific sight to behold.

"Who… who did this to you!?", he squeaked.

"My mother.", she replied, before bursting into tears.

"What!? Why would she do something like… THIS!? Was she trying to kill you!?"

"She- she's always been like this.", she choked out between sobs. "I just can't take it anymore!"

"Why are you letting her do this to you!?"

"What am I supposed to do? I can't do anything about it!"

"You need to call the cops, call someone!"

She stared at him wide-eyed. "Oh I can' do that! She's my mother!"

"She's going to freaking kill you! You need to do something!", he yelled angrily.

"B-but she's my mother!"

"Who cares if she's your mother? Just because she's your parent means she's allowed to brutalize you? That's insane!", he yelled. "Listen to me. You need to do something before it's too late."

"I- I can't! I have nobody else other than her."

"Olivia! You were the first friend I've ever had. I can't just stand here and let you wait and die! If you won't do it, I will!"

"John, please… just – I can't. Please.", she cried.

John stared at her, horrified. If he had to choose between what Olivia was suffering through and the constant neglect he had to deal with, he would have gladly chosen neglect. He needed to do something, and hopefully it worked.

"Should I help you get home then?"

"No. No, she'll hit me even more if I brought someone home."

"Come over to my place, I can try to get you some help."

"I- I can't… If I don't go home, my mom's going to beat me again…"

"Olivia…", he pleaded. "I really don't want the next time I see you to be in an obituary."

"Okay…", she said painfully.

John helped her walk to his house, hurriedly. He didn't even realize that this was the first time he was bringing a friend home. That didn't matter in the slightest at the moment. Her life was in danger, and he needed to save it. His friends had shown they'd do it for him, now it was his turn to show them the same resolve. By the time they had made it to John's house, Olivia could barely stand.

"Are you okay!?", he panicked. *'What am I supposed to do!?'*

"Wait, I'll call my parents!", he said, running towards the phone. His fingers slipped multiple times from panic alone before he managed to call his parents.

"Mom! I need help! Please, come home…"

"John? Did something happen!? Wait right there, we're coming home soon!"

"Sorry… for bothering you…", Olivia said, slouched in a chair.

"Don't be. Wait, I'll get you some water."

John sat down across from her, staring at her in worry. The water seemed to have helped, but she didn't look much better. He began pacing around the room repeatedly. When were his parents going to come home!? Olivia looked like she could pass out any second!

"John are you okay!?", his mother shouted as she ran directly for him.

"It's not me, it's her!"

"Oh… Who is she?"

"She's my friend. She needs help."

"Oh? What kind of friend, John?", his father smiled.

John didn't understand what his father had meant by that. "She was the first friend I've ever made. She needs help!"

They turned around to see Olivia in the couch.

"Oh hello! You must be…", his mother began.

"Olivia", whispered John.

"Yes right, Olivia! How are you?"

"Sorry to disturb you.", she muttered.

"Don't be. You're one of John's friends, you're more than welcome here.", replied his father.

"You must be very hot! You don't need to wear that jacket and scarf in here. I'll help you.", his mother said.

"No wait!", yelled John, but he was too late. His mother shrieked loudly as she saw the bruises and cuts on Olivia. As she stepped back in shock, she almost fell over the table, only to be caught by John's father.

"What's wrong!?", asked John's father.

"Her – she's really hurt! John, you should have called for an ambulance!", she shrieked, picking up her phone.

John's father looked at Olivia before turning to John. "Do you know what happened to her? Who did this?"

John took one last look at Olivia. Even in her condition, she was extremely terrified. She kept mouthing to him the word 'no', but John ignored her. If he listened to her now, she might end up in even more pain. "It was her mother."

"Her WHAT!?", John's mother shrieked. "Her mother did this to her!? Oh sorry, the address is…"

"Yes. Her mom did it, and she was trying to hide the injuries with her scarf and sweater."

"My God! Why would someone do that to their own child!?"

"Because…", Olivia said weakly. "She's been like that ever since she divorced my dad…"

A depressing silence settled in, broken only by a few pained gasps from Olivia as John's mother began trying to dress her wounds as they waited for an ambulance. John's father took this opportunity to drag John out of the living room and into the kitchen.

"John, I wanted to apologize. You might not know why for a long time, but I want you to know how sorry I really am.", he said.

"I know… dad."

"Don't worry about your friend. Your mother and I will take care of it. I promise."

John watched as his parents talked to the paramedic, answering their questions. John had never asked for much, but he pleaded silently to his parents, hoping that they could help her.

John paced around his room. It's been a week since Olivia had went to the hospital and he hadn't heard anything about her since. People had been asking around about her whereabouts, but the only person who knew was John and the two others he's told. But just like he had expected, nobody actually cared enough to ask further. What was he supposed to do now? Was she okay?

"John are you okay?", asked his mother, startling him. He hadn't noticed her standing in the doorway the entire time.

"N-yeah. I'm fine.", he lied. His mother sighed, she had been watching him pace around the room for the last five minutes. It couldn't be any more clearer something was bothering him.

"Does it have to do with the girl–"

"Olivia.", he interrupted.

"Right. Does it have anything to do with her?"

John sat down on the corner of his bed. "Yeah. I wish I could go visit her. I haven't seen her in a long time."

His mother smiled. "Do you like her?"

"Well, she was the first person to ever talk to me and the first person to ever become my friend. I guess I'd say I like her", said John, not understanding what his mother actually meant.

"Why don't you go visit her then?"

John sat straight up. "I can?"

"Of course! Why wouldn't you be?", she responded, stifling a laugh. John on the other hand was blown away by this information. He didn't actually think he could visit her, much less having his mother take him there. He couldn't contain his excitement. It was the first time he's ever visited anyone.

Once his mother started the car, he leapt down the stairs and ran outside towards it. Even in the car he couldn't contain his excitement.

Once his mother parked the car, he immediately dashed out only to realize they hadn't reached the hospital.

"Why are we here?", he asked his mother.

"You don't want to go empty handed, do you?"

"I don't?"

His mother laughed again and led him into the store. As much as he didn't want to admit, he knew very little about his friends liked. His mother thought as much so she bought a box of chocolates and small get-well card.

"Give this to her once you see her.", his mother said. She winked at him, but he still didn't understand what she meant. She's been acting really strange ever since John had said he liked Olivia. Even during the drive to the hospital, she kept looking back at him, smiling.

Once they got to the hospital, his mother waited behind.

"Go, ask the receptionist.", she beckoned. "I don't want to get between you two."

'Okay, which alternate reality did I slip into?', he thought to himself. His mother was acting far too weird for his liking, but he shook off his doubt and walked towards the receptionist.

"Hello.", he mumbled quietly.

"Yes?"

"I'm looking for…", he mumbled again. Only now did he realize what his mother had meant. His face felt as if it was on fire and he quickly turned away from the receptionist.

"I'm sorry, could you speak up?", the receptionist asked.

John couldn't say anything anymore. He was far too embarrassed to even move his face. Luckily for him, his mother had noticed and arrived to help.

"Let's go John.", his mother said, patting him on the back.

"Huh?"

"Olivia's on the third floor, room three twenty-one."

His heart started beating harder than ever. Once they got to the room, the door swung open as Kent and Marcus stepped out. The very sight of them made John's blood freeze. Thankfully, they didn't see him since they left in the other direction. Olivia on the other hand was a dreadful sight. Both of her arms were in casts and was covered in so many bandages it looked as if she was being mummified.

"John?", she croaked.

"Uh… hi?". He looked around and saw a box of doughnuts with a teddy bear sitting atop it so he laid the chocolates and get-well card beside them before rigidly walking out. His mother was waiting right outside, furious.

"What are you doing?", she hissed. "Talk to her!"

John walked back in as rigidly as before. Though her face was bandaged, he could see Olivia's bemused expression. Even he couldn't prevent himself from laughing at how foolish he must have looked.

"How are you?", he asked.

"Fine. Just wish I could move my arms."

"I brought you some chocolate."

"Aww, you shouldn't have. It's nice of you to do so, but I won't be able to reach them!", she laughed. "Same with the doughnuts Kent brought."

"Is your mom here too? She's such a nice person. She even visited me a few times."

"Really?", asked John, surprised.

"Olivia!", blurted his mother, now showing herself from the doorway. "You didn't have to tell him that!"

"Sorry!"

Olivia and his mother began laughing. John couldn't help himself but start laughing as well. He was worried for nothing after all. Though she was bandaged almost beyond recognition, it was nice to see her happy. It was nice to be proven wrong once in a while.

"Olivia! It's time to change your – Oh sorry!", a nurse said.

"It's okay! We don't want to disturb her too much.", said John's mother. "Come John. We'll visit another day."

"Thanks John.", said Olivia.

"For what?"

"For everything."

Chapter 16: The Perfect Opportunity

Mr. Anderson arrived at the school earlier than usual, looking over the grades of the multiple late assignments students were handing in. As the school year came to a close, all the students began panicking. Dozens of assignments from dozens of students. They didn't care for the wellbeing of their teachers. Then again, his peers didn't care for the wellbeing of their students either. Mr. Anderson let out a heavy sigh. He couldn't pretend to be better than his peers or superiors if he did about as much as them about the issues of the school.

He became a teacher to help people, not to be stuck waiting for the worthless administration just for them to do nothing about to rampant bullying and harassment. Many people knew that this school was much better funded than the majority of the schools in the area, so why were there so many problems? Mr. Anderson knew better. Throwing money at something would change nothing, and only a fool thought otherwise. Unfortunately, the entire board was full of those very same fools. Nobody in this god forsaken school cared about the students, not even the other students.

It was over. This year would be his last as a teacher. Worthless administration, useless teachers, contemptible students… education was a hell in which anyone worth their salt was damned to rot within. He had already given up on the ideals that drove him to be a teacher in the first place.

Mr. Anderson continued looking over the assignments, checking whether or not he missed anything. Every single one of these names, ranging from unique to downright generic. They'll all forget how he toiled for their sake, but he wouldn't. How could he forget? How could he forget about Dylan, the menace that was a shining example of how the school system failed the student body? How could he forget Mark, who was so foolish that he didn't bother hiding that he was copying someone else's assignment?

Worst of all, how could he forget John who, despite his average run-of-the-mill name, was the most dangerous monster ever created by the school system. How could one frail, terrified boy transform into a barbaric hooligan that was always an inch away from massacring the entire school at any given moment? Were it not for his friends calming him down, Mr. Anderson wouldn't have been surprised if anything were to happen. There were only three people in the school that had the ability to calm him down. Two of which had their own obligations to fulfill and the one who was closest to him was no longer physically able to attend the school for the remainder of the year. The boy was a ticking time bomb.

Every single name, yet not a single person he could find that had surpassed his low expectations. Though a handful had met them, the majority have fallen short. Mr. Anderson punched their grades into his computer, reaching for another folder of assignments. This one was filled with assignments for a completely different subject. As low as his expectations were for the students, he had zero for his peers. Yet they all had fallen short. They couldn't even organize their own belongings.

There was only one month left in the school year. Surely he could survive one more month… right? Mr. Anderson wasn't going to hold his breath, *unless…*

Another day, another jog towards the school. Despite how early in the day it was, it was still very hot. Summer was approaching and heralded the end of the school year. Everyone was either beginning to mellow out or stressed beyond belief. John could see some people walking into the school, scribbling away at homework assignments that were most likely weeks if not months old.

"Hey MARCUS!", shouted John.

"Oh, what's up?"

"Nothing much. You read the message they gave out the other day?"

"Yeah, but I don't think it's true. There's no way the board of education's going to send a supervisor this late. There's barely a month left in the school year.", shrugged Marcus.

"Well, Mr. Anderson's always complained about how terrible the school was. You never know y'know?"

They didn't have much time to discuss whether or not the information was true when a portly woman stepped out of a car marked with the board's logo into the school.

"You think that was her?"

"Who else would it be? A cow?", Marcus snickered.

Mr. Anderson looked much more cheerful than John had ever saw him. The smile and, when John looked very closely, slight drooling showed how much he relished this day. That woman was definitely someone important if he was this happy.

"Today is going to be a great day! I feel it in my *bones*.", said Mr. Anderson giddily. "Maybe this school will finally be a real school! And I was planning on quitting after this year too… I guess I'll stick around for another year!"

"Why were you planning on quitting, sir?", asked a student.

"Because of you lot. This place killed my drive to be a teacher. Horrible students and even worse faculty.", divulged Mr. Anderson. Everyone stared at him wide-eyed. Of all the teachers to say something along those lines, they never expected *him* to say anything of the sort.

After a brief moment, Mr. Anderson came back to his senses and tried to keep his emotions in check. "Never mind what I just said. You'll see your other teachers are going to be a bit more disagreeable than usual."

Just as he said, the other teachers were completely different. As if they had been supercharged, every teacher moved around like it was their last day in the school. The once sedentary teachers now had eyes on the backs of their head, sniping students who weren't paying attention with detentions. The once free students had suddenly been chained by the newfound authority the teachers were now showing. Even the clownish acts of Dylan's friends hadn't gone unnoticed. By the time it was recess, almost every member of his gang had been given detention.

"The teachers are on a warpath huh?", said Kent.

"I know right? It's crazy how many people have detention. Wonder how long that supervisor woman's planning on, uh, supervising?", wondered Marcus.

"HEY, YOU! NO RUNNING IN THE HALLS!", a teacher barked at a student.

Watching their peers squirm trying not to invoke the wrath of the teachers was hilarious for the students that weren't in danger of punishment, but they knew their time would come soon enough. The ones that were already in trouble were already voicing their opinions on the fat cow that was ruining the last few days of the school year.

Suddenly, John had a most devious idea spring in his mind. A way to finally get vengeance on Dylan for all those times he jumped him. With all of his bolder friends stuck with detention after school, Dylan would be all alone. Never would John be able to get another chance at vengeance. Nobody to help him, everyone to watch. This long, painful chapter of John's life was finally coming to an end.

"DYLAN!", John shouted, shoving his bully from behind.

"What do *you* want?", snarled Dylan.

John began leering at him, smiling menacingly and cracking his fingers and flexing his arms for added effect. "Be ready after school!"

The news would had spread like wildfire among the other students, but they had made sure to keep it out of earshot of the faculty and anyone who could possibly snitch. The two most hated individuals in the entire school were about to rip each other apart. Regardless of who won, it was a great day for everyone.

"No way you're gonna beat up Dylan after school are you?", asked Kent.

"Course I will. I've been waiting so, so, sooooo very long! You don't know how much I'm going to enjoy this.", said John, drooling in anticipation.

"You think you can?"

"He's always surrounded with his friends. Now that they aren't in the picture I'm going to rip him apart, piece by piece."

To Dylan's credit, he wasn't unnerved by what John had said. Despite that, he couldn't act as smug and arrogant as he usually did. Normally he would never care how much one of his victims had changed, but John was a different case. Everyone else would either try to do his bidding or flee upon seeing him, but John never did any of those. He did the exact opposite and stood up to him, the first of his victims to ever do so.

Dylan didn't care much about that though. Instead he thought about John's physical appearance. Dylan used to be larger than John, but John had spent at least the past six months training himself for nothing but getting revenge. Had Dylan also kept up with his training, he could have easily wiped the floor with John, but after making it into the football team he returned to his usual pastime of lounging around and bossing his underlings around. It's not as if he expected someone to ever challenge him to a fight after he had placed the entire student body under his thumb.

Unfortunately for him, he had no choice but to fight and win. John was already unpopular and either disliked or unacquainted with others. Nothing would change for him if he got beaten once more. Dylan on the other hand bullied half of the school, whether directly or indirectly. If John were to beat him up or if he ran, nobody would ever take him seriously ever again.

The only way to ensure his victory would be to fight dirty… and he had the perfect way to do so.

Chapter 17: The Showdown

Every single one of Dylan's victims, whether directly or indirectly, arrived at the park nearby the school. Nobody was going to miss this once in a lifetime chance to see their worst enemy get their comeuppance. As badly as they wanted to record this fight, they made sure to keep it contained in their memory only. Having their savior be expelled would defeat the purpose of the fight.

John stood in the middle of the crowd waiting for Dylan to show up. If he didn't, Dylan would lose his intimidation. If he arrived, Dylan would be embarrassed in front of dozens of students. If he brought a weapon or brought friends, he would also be embarrassed. The only way for him to get out of this unscathed would be to beat John in front of all these people.

Much to John's chagrin, Dylan wasn't terrified, nor did he look at all like he was shaken. He seemed far too calm for someone surrounded by people who wished him dead on every side.

"You're late. Busy writing your will?", mocked John.

Dylan didn't respond. He threw his bag down onto the dirt and walked towards John. Only now did Dylan really see the difference in build between them. If he wasn't planning on fighting dirty, he might have backed out of this fight. Being laughed at for not fighting would be one thing but being beaten bloody and laughed at for getting beaten so would have been worse.

"Dylan, y-you aight?", asked one of his lackeys that came with him.

"Why wouldn't I be. It's John. Plus I got, you know."

"Alright then, y-take care, I'm outta here!", panicked the boy, running away.

"What a spineless punk. He knows how bad the beating you're about to get is, and he ran away. Why don't you run away?", said John.

The crowd began jeering and laughing. Yet Dylan remained quiet. He didn't speak a word at all but casually slipped his hands into his pockets.

John hammed up every single line. Dylan was quiet, but in John's eyes he was squirming in fear. He walked up to Dylan, puffing out his chest and trying to appear as large as possible.

"What're you going to do you little b- ", said John.

Just as quick Dylan whipped his hand out of his pockets and threw something directly at John's face. John had barely managed to close his eyes in time before most the dirt, sand, or whatever fine material Dylan had thrown at him, had hit them. But the distraction worked as Dylan immediately punched John square in the face. From the distance and angle, the others couldn't see what Dylan had thrown, but their mocking began dying out as he began pummeling John with his fists and feet.

Blinded and disoriented, John swung his arm out trying to grab the general direction of where the hits were coming from. As soon as he grabbed something, he used his other hand to grab Dylan's shirt and headbutted his face as hard as he could. Despite being blinded, the cheering of the crowd let him know that he had dealt a devastating blow. John opened his eyes slightly to see the furious Dylan trying to punch him in the eye. If he wasn't going to play nice, then neither would John. As soon as Dylan's fist contacted his face, John's leg moved up and -

"OOOOOH!", everyone groaned as John's knee rose up full force and hit Dylan in the crotch. But John wasn't done. He grabbed Dylan's head in a hold while repeatedly pounding it with his other hand. This wasn't just to cause him pain, he needed to thoroughly embarrass him in front of all these people. John began tugging at his hair, his ears, anything that looked like it hurt more. He needed Dylan to cry out in pain, to scream for help! For if he did, then John would have truly won.

But Dylan wasn't some thug that just relied on intimidation like the rest of his lackeys. He knew how to fight. He slipped his leg between John's and tried to push him over. All he needed to do was get John on the floor so he could pin him and beat his face in. In his attempt at getting John to trip, he had managed to free himself of his hold. The brute strength and intimidation his lackeys loved using had no power here. John had proven he was physically stronger than him, but John knew exactly what he planned on doing. After all those times Dylan used him as a punching bag how could he not? Dylan had beaten his various methods of inflicting pain into him. Before Dylan could do so himself, John tackled him with all of his weight.

Dylan's plan had completely backfired. Now it was *he* who was pinned under John's weight. For the first time ever, Dylan was cowering! But it wasn't going to save him, the same way John's cowering never saved him. John swung his arms, mauling Dylan with as much force as he could possibly muster.

"W-wait – ", Dylan rasped as John's fist crashed into his face. But the beating didn't stop there. He kept punching his bully's face over and over, blood now oozing from his broken nose, but John wasn't anywhere near done. All that pent up rage, all those beatings, were being paid back tenfold. With every other punch, Dylan's arms resisted less and less until they were completely flat on the ground.

John looked down at his greatest foe laying spread-eagle on the ground and unconscious. All the hatred that was in John's body had been emptied out in that five-minute fight. As the realization sunk in, his body began to feel lighter and lighter, HE HAD WON! Almost everyone began yelling, cheering, or raging at the result of the fight. The few of Dylan's supporters that had come to witness the fight were panicking, some even crying. He even saw Luke in the crowd, devastated. They had just witnessed their reign of terror over the school come to an end.

He looked down once more at the pitiful body of Dylan who was now pretending to be unconscious. The dream that he so desperately wished for had finally come to fruition. Unfortunately, he didn't get to savor his victory over Dylan.

"Oh snap, there're teachers coming here! Everyone, RUN!", someone shouted. John ran home, heart pounding like crazy. Before this moment he never saw Dylan as a person, but as something chaining him down. But today he had finally broken those chains.

He was *free.*

Epilogue: Smith's Identity

Many days had passed since Dylan's defeat at the hands of his once weakest victim. When everyone had ran from the park the only one remaining was Dylan. The teachers had found Dylan and punished him for fighting with a suspension. He was already going to miss a few days due to his injuries, so the punishment was little more than an insult on top of those injuries. Despite losing the fight, having lost most of his 'friends', and his popularity tanking, Dylan didn't mention who had beaten him so brutally. Maybe out of embarrassment or how nobody would believe the boy he gloated about bullying would be the one who did him in, nobody knew.

'Sounds like he won't be bothering anyone for quite some time.', messaged Olivia.

'I don't think he will. How're your arms doing?', he replied.

'They say the scars might stay for a long time, maybe even forever, but they've healed! I might be able to see you guys in person next year!'

'But I still have a ton of work to catch up on. Catch you later!'

After what had happened with Olivia, she had missed the remainder of the year. Her mother had been arrested for child abuse and she ended up with her father. Though John hadn't met either of her parents, her father seemed much nicer than the demon her mother was after seeing how much better Olivia had been doing.

John was sat in his chair, where this journey began. The weak and antisocial boy six months ago had evolved into a strong, outgoing young man that was outgrowing the chair he currently sat in. It was almost cathartic for him, but one thing was still eating at him. The journey was ending, but the one person that was there from the beginning was nowhere in sight! Where on earth was Smith? If he was right then…

"What ever happened to casting off the chains that held you back?", asked the familiar voice he was waiting for.

"I did more than cast them off, I broke them.", answered John, smiling now that he had finally achieved peace with himself. "But you already knew why I did that didn't you?"

"So you know?"

'Well now it's pretty obvious. I guess all that time I just wanted someone who cared.'

John laughed, remembering everything he had gone through this school year. The training, the brawling. The friends he made. The hardships he suffered…

None of that would have happened if he hadn't managed to delude himself into believing Smith was more than just a figment of his imagination.